Alec Birri served thirty years with the UK Armed
Forces. He commanded an operational unit that
experimented in new military capabilities classified at
the highest level (Top Secret Strap 3) and it is this that
forms the basis of his novels.

Although semi-autobiographical, for national security
and personal liberty reasons, the events and individuals
portrayed have to be fiction, but are still nonetheless in
keeping with his experiences.

www.alecbirri.com

CONDITION

BOOK TWO

ALEC BIRRI

Matador
9 Priory Business Park,
Wistow Road, Kibworth Beauchamp,
Leicestershire. LE8 0RX
Tel: (+44) 116 279 2299
Fax: (+44) 116 279 2277
Email: books@troubador.co.uk
Web: www.troubador.co.uk/matador

ISBN 978 1785898 778

British Library Cataloguing in Publication Data.
A catalogue record for this book is available from the British Library.

Printed and bound by CPI Group (UK) Ltd, Croydon, CR0 4YY
Typeset in 11pt Aldine by Troubador Publishing Ltd, Leicester, UK

Matador is an imprint of Troubador Publishing Ltd

PROLOGUE

'Please don't hurt me, Uncle Joe.'

'Don't be silly, Juan. It's only a haircut.'

'But I feel funny.'

Uncle Joe switched on the clippers and began cutting. 'That's because you ate too many of the chocolates I gave you.'

Juan could still taste the bitterness of them. He didn't think they were very nice. Not as nice as the ones Uncle Joe gave him yesterday. The six-year-old screwed his face up as the blades passed over his head.

Juan hated having his hair cut. It was like going to the hospital or visiting the dentist. All three scared him enough to make him cry, but not this time. Uncle Joe said the special chocolates would make sure he wasn't frightened and he was right. They tasted horrible and made Juan feel woozy, but he wasn't scared and that made him a big boy now.

He liked Uncle Joe. All the children did. He wasn't their real uncle, of course, but everyone called him that because he was so kind, especially if you had something wrong with you.

Juan's big sister once had a tummy upset, which must

have hurt because she was always crying about it. It upset his Mama and Papa too especially Papa who got very angry – he got angry a lot. Juan had to leave the room when that happened, which was fine because Papa's shouting scared him. Juan could still hear him though and he found out Maria must have been really ill because the doctors couldn't help and Uncle Joe had to. He was the only one who could 'get it out'. Uncle Joe could do anything. Juan wondered if he knew God. He lived in a big house on top of a big hill so maybe he was God?

Juan didn't know what happened after that, but his sister must have got better, because Papa stopped shouting about it. It still hurt Maria though because she carried on crying afterwards – especially when Juan or one of her other brothers hugged her. But Papa said she was being silly, while Mama said nothing. She just prayed. She prayed a lot and especially when Maria was first ill. Whatever it was must have been bad.

Everyone in the village knew that if you had something wrong with you, Uncle Joe was the one you went to see and especially if it was something the other doctors couldn't mend. He must have had special medicine or healing. Maybe Uncle Joe was Jesus?

Uncle Joe had candy, too, and when he came out of his big house to go down the big hill into the village, all the children would run up to meet him. They knew it was naughty, and their mamas scolded them for doing it, but Uncle Joe always gave them something nice, so it was worth a hiding. Of course, what the children really wanted to do, was go to the big house.

This was because some lucky ones had been ill or hurt badly enough for their mamas to have to take them there – just like Juan's big sister. Pedro said he broke his arm on purpose so he could go, but nobody believed him. Anyway, he said it was *full* of candies. Jars and jars of every sweet you could think of: chocolate, liquorice, aniseed, sherbet; every candy that had ever been invented. Just thinking about that made Juan laugh and when Uncle Joe asked if he and his brothers would all like to go to the big house and try some, well, they just couldn't believe their luck. All they had to do was keep it a secret. Juan liked keeping secrets. It made him feel special. Uncle Joe said they were *all* special.

Juan tried to think of what happened next. All the boys went to the big house as promised and he could remember the chocolates and how they all said they didn't taste very nice, but nothing after that. He wondered what was happening now. He knew he was having his hair cut but couldn't understand why as Mama only did it last week.

He had cried like a baby then, but he was smiling now. Uncle Joe was amazing. Being brave about the haircut meant Juan was one of the older boys now, which was important. Mama would be angry if she knew they had all gone to Uncle Joe's big house without her. If she found out, she would beat them all before making a sign of the cross and praying for their forgiveness. Juan hoped Uncle Joe really was Jesus.

Juan could feel himself floating above the chair and

he giggled. 'Wooo-weee! I'm flying!' He rolled his head from side to side.

'Now, keep still, or you really will get hurt.'

Juan tried to. Honestly, he did, but he was having so much fun it was difficult to stay still for long. He loved Uncle Joe. If he wasn't God or Jesus, then he was the nicest person in the whole world. Juan didn't care about the nasty *or* the nice candy; what he wanted more than anything was a papa who didn't shout at him and Uncle Joe never did that.

As with each of the brothers, the doctor had to steady the little boy's face with a hand to finish shaving his head.

Soon, all the children were sedated and prepared for the next stage.

Mengele switched off the clippers and plugged in an electric drill.

PART ONE

1977

CHAPTER ONE

Detective Sergeant Emiliano Vazquez studied the latest missing persons' list, and compared it to the previous copy. It was twice the length. How the police were expected to investigate them all, he didn't know.

He made a calculation.

'1995.'

The desk officer looked up. 'What?'

'At this rate, in eighteen years' time the entire population of Argentina will have gone missing.' He turned the lists towards the corporal. 'So if it's 1977 now, we'll *all* be dead by 1995.' The officer shrugged and carried on reading his newspaper.

Emil put the lists down and deleted those names he had previously investigated – pointless going over those again as any backhanders from the families would have long since dried up, even if the bodies had yet to be found.

It was always a body. Never a case of mistaken identity, a runaway returned home or released kidnap victim. If you went missing in South America these days, that's how you stayed.

But then, chasing ghosts was all the police could

do, and thanks to the military junta's determination to wipe out the communists, there was always a plentiful supply of those desperate to find out why their fathers, sons and occasionally, daughters had stopped coming home. Families themselves sometimes disappeared, but the investigation of them was strictly off limits to a newly promoted sergeant in the *Policia Federel Argentina*. They invariably involved government-backed militias and messing with them was one surefire way of finding yourself on a list – of one.

Emil set about reducing the new names to the few he would 'investigate'. This was the tricky bit – trying to work out who was likely to pay the most without stepping on any toes further up within the police, never mind some mob with connections. It meant there was never any decent money to be had of course – the wealthy took their bribes straight to the top, but there was always the odd doctor or solicitor's family that could be good for a few pesos.

That took some investigating of its own, however and it started with a process of elimination. He struck his pen through each of the peasants – no money there. Likewise, he deleted those identities with known communist connections or other criminal records, before moving on to the laborious but potentially lucrative part; a methodical search of the Buenos Aires telephone directory.

That took care of the rest of his shift, and by four o'clock he had six names – all professionals: a dentist, solicitor, teacher and three businessmen. He could take a month's salary from that little lot in just a day if the families lived close enough. He put down the notepad and walked over to a map of the city.

'Good work, Sergeant.'

Emil's heart sank and he mouthed an obscenity before turning back to face his boss.

Inspector Gomez had the notepad in his hand, and was studying the names. 'But I think it would be better if I dealt with these. The families of dentists and solicitors can be very judgmental of junior police officers and I might be able to get more out of them.' He looked at his Sergeant. 'If you know what I mean.'

Emil knew what he meant alright – the higher the rank, the more the families were prepared to shell out, but he would be lucky to receive the equivalent of a day's pay let alone a month once the inspector had taken his cut.

The desk officer grinned at Emil's misfortune and the inspector pounced on it. 'What are you smiling at? Get back to work!' The corporal struggled to stay on his seat. Gomez motioned for Emil to join him in his office and closed the door once they were inside.

'It's called 'RHIP', Sergeant – rank has its privileges. I'm sure you'll understand once you get to my position.' He offered Emil a cigarette but then withdrew the packet before he had a chance to take one. 'Or perhaps you reckon on having enough money to retire before then?' The packet was offered again.

Emil hesitated before taking the Marlboro. His boss lit it, and then his own.

The young sergeant recognised a veiled threat when he encountered one. It wasn't that he feared any physical harm or indeed disciplinary action – selecting what to investigate based on the potential of bribes was endemic within the police – no, what worried him most was being shut out of any future opportunities if his loyalty could be called into doubt. Ensuring his boss had received a fair share of gains in the past was academic. For the first time his superior had seen what Emil was planning. If the inspector did carry out the 'investigations' himself and managed to get more than expected, then that could spell trouble for Emil. RHIP indeed.

Emil became contrite. 'No, Sir. I've always known where I stand with you and would like to think my sergeant would do the same for me when, er, I mean, *if* I get to become an inspector.'

Gomez ignored the answer and studied the names again. His lips moved in silence as if working something out. To Emil's surprise, the notepad was then offered back to him. But he couldn't take it.

'I need you to investigate something else first.' Gomez released his end of the pad and walked over to a map of the country. Emil groaned to himself as the inspector pointed to a location in the foothills of the Andes – a good two days' drive away. Emil became positively nauseous when he found out what he had to do.

'There's an abortion clinic operating under the guise of an orphanage in the village of Ariloch.' He turned to his junior. 'Go there, find out what's going on, arrest and charge those responsible, and shut it down.'

Emil was grateful for the return of the list, but not with what was basically a local matter. Given the distance, a week would be needed and he had bills to pay now – zero bribes in peasant country. Communist guerrillas hid out in those hills too and army or police; they didn't care who they killed. He tried to get out of it.

'What's wrong with the local police? Why aren't they dealing with it?'

Gomez gave a look that indicated he didn't tolerate his orders being questioned but answered it anyway. 'They were until one of the mothers decided to abort her children *after* they were born and I believe that's called murder so homicide has become involved.' He regarded Emil with suspicion. 'Unless of course you don't want to do any *real* police work?'

Of course Emil did and that included risking his life but not if the infanticides turned out to be at the hands of some inbred incapable of understanding her actions. Packing her off to a nuthouse was hardly a result to be proud of and certainly not one worth dying for. It might technically be murder, but there were way more serious crimes than the mercy killing of some half-dead incestuous runts. The people were little more than animals up there, anyway.

Emil's sigh was more visible this time. 'Is there a pathologist's report?'

The inspector burst out laughing. 'The country's at war, Emil. We're dealing with a dozen bodies a week thanks to the antics of the Reds. There aren't enough pathologists for that let alone the dead sprogs of a village idiot. Not that you need a medical degree to recognise a bullet through the head.'

It seemed to dawn on Gomez the risk he was asking his sergeant to take. 'Look, I tell you what. Give me back the list and I'll make a start on it. It will give you something to look forward to while you're away. You know I'll be able to make more er, *progress* than you.'

As if Emil had a choice in the matter. For all he knew the abortion clinic was just a ruse to get him out of the way so Gomez could keep the backhanders to himself. Emil tore out the page and handed it over.

'Who's going with me?'

The inspector bit his bottom lip. 'We can't spare anyone at the moment so you'll be on your own.' Emil's eyes widened and was about to protest when his boss interrupted. 'Don't worry, I've arranged for a relay of police and military escorts to get you there and back in one bit.'

The sergeant felt a little better but thought the transport plan bizarre. It was almost as if he had to get there no matter what. Emil was used to strange orders from his boss, especially now the government was having to clamp down so hard but that was usually because some rich family was paying through the nose for protection, but why the same fuss for a bunch of penniless peasants?

Gomez passed him a file. 'Here – you can read up on the case during your journey.' Emil opened it and counted the number of pages – both of them. Barely more than a map and a couple of contact details.

The inspector extinguished his cigarette and opened

the door. He grabbed his sergeant's arm as he was about to leave. 'Some priest will want to give the kids a decent funeral once you're done.' Emil was pulled closer. 'Make sure he buries *everything*.'

CHAPTER TWO

'Sergeant Vazquez?'

Emil stopped and glanced around. He'd already spotted the padre's cassock a couple of hundred metres further down the track, but being recognised out of uniform was worrying. The pastor closed the distance between them and smiled as he stretched out a hand.

'I'm Padre Martin. Welcome to my parish.'

Emil's eyes flitted left and right as if expecting to be ambushed at any moment, but empty scrubland between the two men and the foothills in the distance made that unlikely. He shook the pastor's hand, but Emil was still nervous. He wanted to put a hand on his pistol, but the padre kept a firm hold while expanding on the welcome.

'And on behalf of the people of Ariloch, I hope you enjoy your stay with us.'

He let go. Nothing bad happened, so Emil relaxed a little. 'How did you know it was me?'

The priest laughed. 'Ariloch is twenty miles from the nearest town with little to offer the weary traveller so we don't get many visitors and when we're told to expect one, we like to make him feel welcome. Can I help you with your bag?'

Emil pulled it further up onto his shoulder to indicate he didn't and looked past the padre. He couldn't see the outskirts of the village so guessed there was still some walking to do. The military truck had dropped him a mile or so back so it couldn't be that much further. 'Didn't we arrange to meet in the church?'

The pastor turned his head towards it. The cross on top could be seen in the distance. 'I thought it best to escort you on the final part of your journey. The *Dirty War* has made the villagers nervous and they sometimes don't take kindly to strangers.' He turned back to the policeman. 'Especially if they're military or police, so it might be better if I introduce you as my friend, 'Mr' Vazquez.'

Emil nodded. Fair enough – anything to help break down barriers. His official status would have to be revealed at some stage, though.

The remaining twenty minutes of the journey was spent discussing the extent of guerrilla activity in the area; or at least what the padre had seen or been made aware of. Emil was relieved to hear that although the police station in the town had been attacked, no outsiders had been seen in Ariloch for years.

He still wanted to be in and out as soon as possible, though. 'Mr' Vazquez or not, it was only a matter of time before some enterprising villager decided a few pesos could be made as an informant and even the most pious of priests could be susceptible to that.

They were about to enter the village when Emil spotted someone attempting to hide behind a tree ahead of them. He stopped and took out his gun.

The padre put a hand on top of it. 'It's only Pedro.' He shouted for him to join them. 'It's okay, Pedro, come and meet my new friend.'

Emil holstered the weapon as a boy of about ten, gingerly approached, unable to take his eyes off where the padre's new friend had hidden the pistol from view.

'Say, hello to Mr Vazquez, Pedro.'

One of Pedro's arms was deformed and Emil's natural suspicions became sidelined for pity. He bent down and put out a hand. The boy cowered so Emil leaned forward a little more. The weight of the Browning pushed down on the left side of his jacket, exposing the hand grip. Pedro grabbed it and ran.

'Fuck! Fuck!' Emil dropped his bag and tore off after him as fast as he could. 'Idiot!' he cried out loudly as he quickly became outpaced. The boy was like a human monkey the way he bounded over brooks and fences. He was soon out of sight.

'Fuck!' Emil said again when he stopped in the middle of what appeared to be the village square. He was out of breath and had to place his hands on his knees to recover. 'Stupid, stupid idiot!' He looked at the ground and continued to admonish himself for the rookie mistake.

It was only late afternoon, but the sun was already setting behind the Andes and shadows cast by the villagers edged into his field of view. He looked up. A group of about twenty children stood before him.

The padre caught up and deposited Emil's bag at his feet. He wasn't as out of breath and just needed to mop his brow to recover. 'I'm terribly sorry about that, but don't worry, we'll soon get it back.'

He addressed the children, but in a dialect so thick it was impossible for Emil to understand what was being said. Four of them shot off in different directions. The padre then peered at Emil's bag. 'I hope you have something to reward them with when they return your property.'

Emil thought there was next to no chance of getting his handgun back but then realised his second rookie mistake – not bringing any candy for bribes of his own. He tried to think of what he did have. 'A packet of biscuits?' he said, apologetically.

'That should do nicely.'

Padre Martin then turned to the rest of his flock, and introduced 'Senor' Vazquez to them. At least Emil assumed that was what was being done, as it was conveyed in the same impenetrable local patois. It could have been an instruction to prepare a cauldron of boiling water for all Emil knew.

He pondered that thought. The people of Ariloch might not have been cannibals, but they weren't far from savages, judging by the state of their offsprings' clothes and what they lived in. They even appeared to share their dilapidated accommodation with the chickens and goats he could see milling around. In fact, there didn't seem to be much evidence of a normal community at all. No vehicles to speak of, or any other kind of machinery for that matter.

Emil wondered what they did to earn a crust. If they were farmers, then where were the horses, ploughs and carts? How did they till the land or tend livestock? The few he could see appeared to be little more than pets.

The children Emil assumed to be from the orphanage drew nearer as the padre continued to allay their suspicions of the stranger, giving the policeman a chance to eye the potential witnesses more closely. Not that they would have been reliable in court.

Whatever their roots, years of inbreeding was much in evidence – mainly in and around the children's eyes which were either too close together, or too far apart. It gave some of them an almost frog-like appearance.

Some surgical work had been done to try and ease their plight, but although well intentioned, nearly all had been blighted further by the procedure. Some of the scars ran so deep, parts of the brain must have been removed in the process. Emil tried not to wince at the most severely disfigured.

There was no escaping the impression of a Victorian freak show. Emil was both disgusted and fascinated and couldn't take his eyes from them. That morbidity was soon replaced by pity again, however – along with some considerable guilt – when his interest was rewarded by broad smiles.

The posse of youngsters returned. They appeared to be cradling one thing and dragging another. Pedro was dumped at Emil's feet before an argument began over who should be the one to hand the pistol back.

The young detective fretted as the weapon was pulled

back and forth between the orphans. Padre Martin clapped his hands and they stopped. All the children bar one then groaned as the pastor uttered a few more unintelligible words and the next thing Emil knew, the smallest of the group took hold of the barrel in one hand, the grip in the other and moved towards him with it. Beaming proudly, she raised the pistol up like a peace offering.

Emil took the handgun, removed the magazine and pulled the top slide back to ensure the chamber was empty. The children recoiled in horror as if their Maker were about to strike them down, all except Pedro, who stared in awe at the safety procedure.

Another clap of the hands made everyone turn to the padre. He was polite but firm. 'The children and I would be grateful if you could keep that well out of sight during your visit.'

Somewhat embarrassed, Emil released the slide and placed the pistol back into its holster. He slipped the magazine into a pocket next to it but not before pressing down on the top round to ensure they were all still there. He then zipped the two halves of the jacket up to his neck and forced a smile. It didn't seem to improve the Arilochian's negative concerns. The padre coughed towards the holdall.

'Oh yes, of course!' Emil fell to his knees and rummaged through it, looks of horror turning back to curiosity as he did so. He produced the digestives and the eruption of excitement that caused stunned him. The reverend certainly had the orphans well-disciplined as they calmed just as quickly.

Emil decided to give the packet to the little girl who had returned his handgun. She grinned before moving off to share them amongst her fellow playmates. All except for Pedro.

'He has to learn.' The pastor's Svengali-like grip of his backward community seemed to extend to some pretty rough justice. 'The carrot and the stick play an important part in Ariloch and Pedro knows that. Don't you, Pedro?'

The boy looked at the reverend and then at everyone enjoying the biscuits. He nodded before pulling his withered arm closer to him and getting up to move away.

Emil's compassion returned. Snatching the pistol had been wrong but he still wanted to help Pedro. Emil would like to help all of them, but that was out of the question.

There was something about the boy's gait. 'How old is Pedro?'

'Seventeen.'

'*Seventeen*?'

'Well, I christened him that long ago, so unless my maths has let me down again.'

'But he seems so young.'

'If you don't believe me, you can always check his medical records.' He gestured towards the far side of the village.

Emil squinted in the direction of the setting sun. He could see a hill with what appeared to be a large house silhouetted on top of it. The mention of clinical documentation reminded him of his task.

'I'd better take a look at the crime scene while it's still light.'

Padre Martin turned his head to one side. 'Crime scene?' The little girl approached the pastor with what was left of the biscuits and he knelt down beside her. She offered him one of the last two in the packet.

'There's been no crime. We just want to report a missing person.'

CHAPTER THREE

'What do you mean, "no crime?" What else do you call murder and abortion?'

The padre took one of the biscuits from the packet, broke it in two and gave one of the halves back to the little girl. She hugged him to show her appreciation and the reverend stood back up.

'Same as you I should imagine. But I very much doubt anything so disturbing has happened in Ariloch in a long time.'

The child ran over to the detective and offered him the last digestive. He ignored her and approached the pastor. The girl followed.

'I'm here to investigate infanticide. Are you saying there hasn't been a murder?' The little girl held the packet up to him again. The policeman looked down at her and shook his head.

'Not to my knowledge,' the padre said. 'I'm sorry if you've had a wasted journey.'

Emil glanced at the house on the hill. 'I'll be the judge of that, Padre.' He set out in the direction of it, grabbing his bag on the way. An entourage of children headed by the little girl followed.

The detective mumbled to himself. *'If that bastard Gomez has sent me on some wild goose chase just to get me out of the office so he can grab a week's worth of bribes to himself, I'll fucking kill him when I get back – RHIP my ass.'*

Emil thought about the return journey he would have to undertake. *'If I get back.'* He stopped, as did the children. The little girl tried again, but Emil continued to ignore her.

The padre caught up and Emil raised his latest fear. 'Are you certain there are no communists here?'

The reverend appeared puzzled. 'Absolutely. Like I said, there's nothing here for anybody.'

The contract killing of policemen wasn't unknown. Anyone with the right money and connections could have it done, especially with so many militias – government backed or not – out there with something to prove. But Emil was hardly a prime target. The detective had always been meticulous in his duties and especially when dealing with the darker side of it but the informers and other seedy types he plied for information relied equally on him for bungs in return and he'd never reneged on those.

They didn't have the connections anyway, and even if Gomez had decided his newest sergeant couldn't be trusted after all, surely he wouldn't have Emil killed for it? And why in the middle of nowhere? If his boss were that desperate to get rid of him, he could do it himself down some dark alley and blame it on muggers. Emil tried ridding himself of the more fanciful conspiracy theories.

The building was beginning to take on the appearance of a haunted house as the sun set behind the mountains, so Emil increased the pace of his final steps, and cast a detective's eye over the scene as he approached.

Although the European design wouldn't be conspicuous in some of the more affluent suburbs of Buenos Aires, the house stood out in Ariloch and especially the condition it was in – almost new compared to the neglected and ramshackled sheds passing as accommodation in the rest of the village. Even the church didn't look as well maintained. The garden had been neglected by comparison with the swings and roundabouts that once made up a playground much in disrepair. The children fought with each other to show off on them when they noticed his interest. All except one very determined little girl, whose arm now appeared permanently outstretched towards him.

Emil was about to refuse her again when to his surprise the front door was opened from the inside. A young woman in her mid-twenties stood before him.

It struck him straight away how different she was from the others. The same genetic Pampas roots, mixed with southern European blood, but none of the physical abnormalities or medical complications of the children were evident. He was wondering if that contrast extended to her mental health when the way she spoke seemed to answer that.

'Good afternoon, Mr Vazquez. Welcome to Uncle Joe's house.'

The polite delivery of her perfect Spanish made him

realise something else. She was pretty too. For a peasant, of course.

Father Martin climbed the steps of the porch and stood next to her, as did the children.

'May I present Ariloch's most famous citizen? This is Senorita Maria Fierro.' The pretty young woman smiled which made Emil blush for some reason. The children giggled. 'And we're very proud of her – she's going to be a doctor one day.'

Maria scoffed at both the description and hopes the pastor had for her, and stepped towards the police officer. 'I'm just an orderly at the local hospital.' She put out a hand to greet him. 'If you can call twenty miles away 'local'.'

Emil shook her hand. But he couldn't shake the feeling something was wrong. A hospital orderly? In a house where abortions took place?

'What are you doing in this house, Miss Fierro?'

She glanced at her priest. 'Making sure it's clean and tidy in case Uncle Joe returns.' The padre corrected her.

'*When* he returns.' Maria didn't argue.

'Who's "Uncle Joe"?'

Maria opened her mouth to speak, but the pastor interrupted. 'Only the saviour of these good people.' He raised his hands to the heavens. 'And when God sees fit to release him from whatever greater good his healing hands are required to do elsewhere, he shall return to complete his work here.' Two of the children moved next to the reverend. He smiled and placed a hand on each of their misshapen skulls.

Emil continued to question Maria. 'You commute to the hospital every day?' She laughed and the way it lit up her face made him blush again.

'Of course not. It's much too far, but I try to come back to my birthplace as often as I can.' She looked down the hill towards the rest of the village. Her eyes seemed to mist over. 'Not that there's much to come back to in Ariloch these days.' She knelt down and put her arms around the youngsters closest to her. 'Just the children.'

Emil thought the scene very strange – a tall, middle-aged priest and a pretty young woman surrounded by a litter of misshapen inbred children, all smiling at him. He firmed his determination.

'Show me the house!' Maria gave him a look. For some reason Emil thought he ought to add 'please' so he did. She smiled again and beckoned him to enter.

The door opened into a hallway, lit naturally by a glass skylight from the floor above. The first of that night's stars could be seen through it so Emil flicked on the light switch. Nothing happened.

'Would you like me to start the generator?' Despite his refusal to believe a crime had been committed, the reverend still seemed keen to help with police enquiries.

The visitor looked at his hosts. 'Is there mains electricity in the village?' Emil had guessed the answer to that halfway through saying it.

'No, but there's a telephone in the church.' Father Martin's departing reply indicated it was the only utility. All the children, bar one, followed him outside to where Emil assumed the house's power supply must be. He took a torch out of his bag and switched it on. Pictures lined the walls in the hallway and the beam was passed over them. Emil guessed Uncle Joe to be a first or second generation European as they were all landscapes from that part of the world. Scenes of the countryside, ornamental gardens and storm-hit coastlines predominated.

The housekeeper and the persistent little girl followed him into a reception room. Emil noticed the child take a firm hold of Maria's skirts as they did. She was uncomfortable and he wondered why.

The European theme continued, with dark wood panels lining the walls and furniture that plainly belonged to someone with not just taste but money and even status – all the chairs were studded in burgundy leather and ornate occasional tables were positioned between them. A heavy ashtray lay in the centre of each. Emil stepped onto the plush carpet, and recalled a smoke-filled room at an ambassador's residence he once waited on as a cadet. A carved marble mantelpiece dominated this room too and he pictured the mysterious uncle leaning on it with a glass of brandy in one hand and a cigar in the other, chuckling to himself over the money to be made from his sickening trade.

He looked at Maria. Surely, such a sweet girl couldn't be Uncle Joe's accomplice? Emil had only just met her, but it would crush what little faith he had in humanity if she was. He suppressed the thought by pretending to examine the expensive drapes framing the tall windows that overlooked the village. The contrast between the two worlds was quite staggering. The idea of some butcher enjoying this lavish lifestyle while the Arilochians struggled to survive just a couple of hundred metres below, made him seethe. He was beginning to understand the communists' point of view.

Not that sympathy would do him any good if they got their hands on him. The thought made him speed up his investigation. He opened one of two doors that led from the room into what turned out to be a short corridor before a kitchen.

Maria lit a candle as she and the little girl followed. The child began whimpering and clung on more to the housekeeper for support but she couldn't be consoled. There was something she didn't like and her increasing concerns told Emil he was getting close to what it was – kitchens were where nearly all illegal abortions took place.

Like the reception room before it, the kitchen was immaculate with the long table in the middle bearing evidence of having been scrubbed – it was still wet. Emil wondered what had taken place there. Copper pots, pans and other utensils hung at various points throughout and spotless crockery adorned extensive wooden shelves. The pretty housekeeper had ensured this room was ready for the owner's return, too.

Keeping an eye on the little girl's reactions, Emil began opening the drawers, expecting an increase in her distress to give away the location of the tortuous tools he was looking for. He hated the idea, but if anything even remotely capable of tearing a foetus out of a woman appeared, Emil would arrest Maria there and then – regardless of the 'uncle's' whereabouts.

As anticipated, the child became more agitated the further Emil progressed so he was somewhat surprised to find the last drawer empty. He scanned the four corners of the kitchen before biting his bottom lip in frustration. The kitchen's function appeared to be exactly that. He took hold of the door handle to the next room. It was locked.

The little girl let go of Maria, and screamed as she ran to Emil. The biscuit packet was still in her hand and he was about to lose his temper with it when she wrapped her arms around his legs and to his amazement, lifted him away – her strength for someone so young and small was remarkable. Floods of tears made her speech unintelligible, but it was clear she wanted him well away from whatever lay behind that door.

Maria put the candle down and rushed to prise her away. Her demeanour had changed. 'We don't go in there.' She reached into the pocket of her apron and gave Emil a key. The child bawled into Maria's shoulder as they retreated back through the house.

The detective unlocked the door. Like the rest of the building, what lay beyond was dark with his torch lighting just the top steps of what led down to some kind of basement. Unlike the rest of the house however, a layer of dust covered them and he had to wipe away cobwebs to get to a light switch. Expecting the generator to burst into life at any moment, he flicked it down and began to descend.

Emil had only taken a couple of steps when it hit him – the smell. A faint but unmistakable mix of blood and disinfectant identical to the much stronger odour that pervades every operating theatre. Nothing could be seen, but there was no doubt in his mind; this was where the atrocities took place, but when? Not recently; the constant need to remove ancient spider works from his face told him it was a long time ago and probably years.

He paused to sweep the blackness with the flashlight when it occurred to him the uncomfortable but familiar scents masked a third. Something not immediately identifiable but just as foreboding. Not being able to see what lay ahead was both frustrating and fearful. His heart raced with trepidation.

Continuing down, a step at a time, the torch eventually illuminated the floor at the bottom. Emil traced the pool of light along its surface until the base of a cabinet appeared. He raised the beam up – senses now pitched perfectly to identify even the smallest of clues. Which was probably why the shock of what Emil saw next made him drop the torch.

Although dead, the contents of the glass jar appeared to scream the moment it was illuminated. The grotesque head of the creature inside even seemed to turn towards Emil as if wanting to convey the full horror of what it had suffered.

If it could be called a head. The flashlight had extinguished the moment it hit the floor but Emil's mind's eye continued to the see the disturbing details: oversized eyes, non-existent nose and ears, a mouth open so wide it seemed to detach the misshapen skull from the additional limbs and externally developed organs that made up what was supposed to be a body. If this poor creature had been born naturally, it didn't live for long.

Emil's battle to fight or flight had begun the moment he shocked himself into darkness and was about to be resolved when he heard the distant sound of a diesel engine being started. The lights came on.

Imminent panic was replaced by instant disbelief. The sudden brightness caused Emil to squint, but that did little to lessen the effect of what row upon row, and tier upon tier of identical glass jars had on him. He now realised what the third smell was – embalming fluid.

Every transparent container had either an under or overdeveloped aborted foetus or stillborn child in various states of preservation. Why? Why keep them? The other illegal abortion clinics the police busted either flushed the results down the lavatory, used incineration or tossed the remnants into the nearest dust cart – they certainly didn't keep the evidence, let alone preserve it.

He made an estimate of their number – it ran into the hundreds when he realised the jars were stored at least two to three deep. There must have been more villagers on those shelves than in the local cemetery – the figure certainly exceeded those still alive and like the living, their appearance both fascinated and repulsed. Emil forced himself away to investigate the rest of the basement.

Even to his untrained eyes he could see the cellar was more than well equipped for the relatively simple procedure of abortion. Although old and uncared for, the sophistication would put many a modern hospital to shame: a proper operating table with the correct lighting above, various electronic monitors, bottles of gas and masks for anaesthesia. It even seemed to double as a laboratory – test tubes and similar glassware sat on the surrounding surfaces along with Bunsen burners and a microscope. He spotted a trolley of surgical instruments and pulled open the top drawer.

'Bingo,' he said out loud when what he'd been looking for turned up. He gave the other drawers a cursory glance before lifting the lid of an autoclave. It contained an electric drill.

Emil was thinking about what to bag and tag when his attention was drawn by what appeared to be a dentist's chair in the corner of the room. It had some kind of frame attached to the back, giving it the appearance of a reject from a ladies' hairdressing salon. It was on wheels so he pulled it further into the light for a better view.

As with a salon's hairdryer, the frame was meant to fit over a person's head. What had that got to do with abortion? He recalled the orphan's disfiguring scars.

The frame had various guides, lugs and attachment points for surgical instruments. Narrow tubes extended uniformly out and around it with clamps at the base that made it clear they were designed to slide down and come into contact with the wearer's skull. Their internal diameter piqued his curiosity further and he went back to the steriliser. He picked up the electric drill and introduced the bit it contained to the end of one. It complained against a touch of rust, but other than that, passed through the tube perfectly.

Emil withdrew the drill, returned it to the autoclave and then walked back over to the macabre collection. He selected one of the jars and wiped the film of neglect from it. The head of what could be seen inside hadn't been drilled but it bore the evidence of forced intrusion – the brain was exposed and in a state that even a layman like him could see was little short of butchery.

He chose another. It was the same. And another. He skipped a few levels with the intention of using random selection to confirm all the preservations had been similarly defiled but then realised the trauma was reducing in severity. It became more methodical – and calculated. The exposed brains of the early jars progressed to gaping holes in others, then less crudely designed access points to incisions that seemed almost delicate in the craniums of later specimens. The surgeon was finessing his skill.

But then something more than just visually disturbing became apparent.

Along with the clumsiness of the early attempts, the physical appearance of each cadaver seemed to improve too. Not enough to be pleasing to the eye by any stretch of the imagination, but enough to show that whatever had been done to the brain, appeared to result in some kind of physical change to at least one of the poor victim's features.

The jars weren't in any random order; their placement seemed to reflect increasing knowledge of not only how the brain worked, but how it could be manipulated to affect development. Emil looked at the chair again. It was clearly meant for much older 'specimens'. He wondered what the mysterious uncle had managed to achieve before he went missing.

Emil had no idea how, why or what had been done in the basement, but he doubted selfless altruism towards the people of Ariloch was behind it. He stood back and looked at the wall of dusty, web-covered specimen jars and the story of artificial creation they seemed to tell.

Maybe the orphans weren't inbred at all. Maybe they'd been made that way.

CHAPTER FOUR

Emil backed towards the basement steps and sat down. He lit a cigarette.

'Magnificent, aren't they?'

The sudden appearance of the padre caused Emil to drop the packet. He picked it up and spun round. 'Magnificent? You're joking, aren't you? This place is straight from a horror movie – *Frankenstein*!'

Padre Martin descended the steps, unable to take his eyes off the display. He seemed to be in an almost trance-like state.

'Oh no – Mary Shelley created a fictional monster that begat another fictional monster. Our Lord God in his infinite wisdom has once again seen fit to send us his son.' He turned to the detective. 'And as the good book foretells, Jesus has returned to raise the dead for all eternity.'

Emil took a step back. The padre's words had left him temporarily lost for any of his own. He regripped the reality that appeared to elude the pastor. 'Father, whatever has been done in this basement, *Jesus* had nothing to do with it.' He pointed to the hundreds of prematurely terminated lives. '*That* is pure evil.'

The padre regarded Emil as if he were naïve to the situation. 'Don't be deceived by their appearance, Sergeant.' He turned back towards what a Second Coming apparently results in. 'You and I would have been just as displeasing to the eye at their stage and we don't look too bad now, do we?'

The policeman put a hand to his brow as if trying to make sense of the statement. 'Are you saying those poor creatures are actually alive?!'

'Of course not, but they soon will be.' Emil was rendered speechless again. The padre seemed to sympathise with him. 'Forgive me. I know it's a lot to take in and as a committed Christian my passion can sometimes come across as overzealous, but what has happened here and will happen again is truly a miracle.' He genuinely appeared to believe the absent 'uncle' was God's son. 'And when Uncle Joe returns, he will lead us *all* into the kingdom of Heaven.'

The padre approached the chair and ran his fingers over the cage-like device. 'Just as he did with Maria's brothers.'

For the first time, Emil picked up on something that could have some sense behind it – albeit just as disturbing. 'Brothers?'

'Oh yes.' Martin pushed one of the tubes down through the frame. 'They're in the caring hands of Our Lord now.' He carved a sign of the cross in mid-air.

'Padre Martin? Where *are* Maria's brothers?' The padre closed his eyes to pray. Emil was in no mood for any spontaneous acts of faith no matter how important they were to the worshipper. 'I said: WHERE ARE THEY?'

'I've already told you, but I assume you're referring to their mortal remains.' He looked towards the top of the basement's steps. 'They're in the church. Their mother is keeping vigil over the coffins until I perform the funerals tomorrow.'

Emil threw what was left of the Marlboro onto the floor and repacked his holdall. He went to retrieve the torch but the priest was holding it.

'Try not to interrupt *her* prayers, Sergeant – the forgiveness of sins is important.' He switched on the flashlight and shone it in Emil's face. 'I wonder if anyone will be there to do the same for you when your time comes?' The torch was handed over.

Emil dusted himself down and got out of the house. He was about to head straight to the church when he realised Maria was waiting for him at the front door. At least that was the impression. The outside air temperature had dropped ten degrees and Maria drew the coat she was wearing tighter around her.

'Don't you ever stop being a policeman?'

So much for the secrecy of 'Mr' Vazquez. Emil was about to say, 'no' but decided to commiserate with her first – no matter how false his stress might make it sound. 'I'm sorry for your loss, Miss Fierro.' The condolence had all the sincerity of a card sharp.

'I guess the answer to my question is, 'No'.' She turned on her heels and headed to the church.

Other than a campfire and feeble glow of the

occasional candle through a window, the route was in darkness so Emil used the flashlight to guide their way. He sensed she didn't want him too near her, so walked a pace behind and to the left so the casting of her shadow didn't make the gesture pointless. It meant lighting only her way which risked him stepping into something he'd rather not, but Emil wanted to make some kind of amends and given the circumstances, being unselfish with his torch was probably the only thing he could do. Appropriate or not, there was no escaping her rights might still have to be read.

They passed the campfire where some of the children could be seen making toast. They laughed and teased each other with the sticks used to keep the bread at arm's length. The picture couldn't have been more opposite to the horrors of the basement. Even the persistent little girl appeared to have got over her attempts to keep Emil out of it. A mangled packet could still be seen in her hand and Emil wondered if she might follow him but guessed it was too dark to identify the torchbearer.

There were no adults present at the joyous scene, and it made Emil realise he'd yet to see any since his arrival. In fact, other than the padre, Maria and her mother, he had yet to see, meet or even hear a mention of anyone above teenage years.

'Maria? Where are the adults? I know Pedro is seventeen, but that still makes him a minor so where are all the parents and grandparents?'

Maria stopped and turned to face him. She looked like an ex, annoyed at Emil for forgetting her birthday or something. Her arms were folded tight, but that was probably because of the cold. Emil wanted to put his arm around her.

'There aren't any. They gradually lost faith in Uncle Joe's return and began drifting away years ago. Only the orphans remain now and the church looks after them.' She continued her journey and Emil rushed to ensure the remainder of it was clear.

They entered the building. The interior was in darkness save for an abundance of candles and tea lights that surrounded the altar, and the short aisle that led up to it. Appropriate organ music could be heard and Emil wondered who must be playing when the sound wavered for a moment indicating the tape machine's batteries were running low.

He turned off the torch and accompanied Maria down the aisle. A woman in black knelt in front of six tiny coffins. Six!

Like other second and third world countries, large families weren't unusual in Argentina and especially in remote villages like Ariloch. Disease and malnutrition meant many children were unable to survive birth let alone the journey into adulthood, but six brothers of the same family and all at the same time? Only two things caused that kind of mortality and as the village didn't appear to be suffering from a pandemic…

Emil was wondering what the protocol was for accusing someone of murder during their prayers when his ribs took a jab from an elbow. He mimicked Maria and drew a sign of the cross on his chest. Anyone watching would think they'd been married for years. They took their place in a pew together just as naturally.

Like the majority of Argentinians, Emil was a Roman Catholic but hardly a regular churchgoer. He often took advantage of God's power to forgive, though – usually at the guilt he felt when taking bribes from families that couldn't afford it. The hours he'd spent in a confessional box far outweighed where he was seated now.

Maria's mother was deep in prayer. She had a set of rosary beads clasped between her palms and paused occasionally to stare at a statue of the Virgin while whispering her Hail Marys. She then looked at the coffins which Emil now realised were nothing of the sort – just wooden boxes. Their size meant the brothers couldn't have been much more than toddlers when they died which was strange because Mrs Fierro must have been well into her forties. He put it down to the hill farmers' ability to breed like rabbits.

Emil assumed her to be the 'village idiot' who'd murdered her 'sprogs' – Inspector Gomez plainly didn't think much of the country's less-fortunate citizens. Emil wondered if he could be just as judgmental. Of course not – Maria and her mother were like any other God-fearing family. For peasants of course.

But there was no escaping the law and questions needed answering. Emil checked his watch. The vigil could go on all night. He nudged Maria and the look she gave him more or less confirmed the possibility.

He was wondering how best to interrupt, when

God seemed to do it for him – the tape player's batteries surrendered. The sudden silence caused both women to stop mid-prayer and look up. Emil seized the opportunity and approached the elder of the two.

'Please accept my condolences at such a difficult time, Mrs Fierro.' His ability to convey sympathy hadn't improved. 'I'm Sergeant Vazquez from the Buenos Aires police and I'm here to investiga—'

The woman sprang to her feet and clutched the front of his jacket. 'You've found him? You've found my boy? Please tell me you've found my son?!'

For a moment, Emil wondered if the shock of losing six offspring had been too much for the mother when Maria got up to separate them.

'No, Mama. We've only just reported him missing. The policeman is here to help us.'

Emil was even more confused now – he had assumed the missing person to be the strange 'uncle'. The village of Ariloch was beginning to turn into the proverbial riddle, mystery *and* enigma.

'Excuse my ignorance, Mrs Fierro but did you say your *son* is missing?' Emil turned to the coffins. 'But I thought—' He interrupted himself when the widow broke down. She rested her head on her daughter's shoulder and the tears flowed. Emil didn't know what to make of the look Maria gave him this time.

The door to the church opened and Padre Martin entered. He was carrying something heavy and for a moment Emil thought things were about to get yet more complicated with a *seventh* coffin, when he realised that it was, in reality, a truck battery. It was placed on the ground next to the tape machine.

The padre wiped his hands on his cassock and approached the three of them. 'Take your mother up to the house, Maria. She's hardly eaten a thing in the past two days.' It was a straightforward request and yet imparted in such a compassionate and caring way. Emil envied the reverend that ability – despite his disturbing comments earlier.

Maria encouraged her mother to leave and the door closed behind them on their way out.

'What the hell's going on, Padre?'

The pastor grimaced before making another sign of the cross, closing his eyes and asking his Maker to, 'Forgive this misguided youth.' He opened them again. 'Nothing is *going on*, Sergeant. We regularly get storms which sometimes uncover graves and I'm afraid this time it's the turn of the Fierro family to suffer the pain of a reburial.'

His explanation was plausible. Most communities grew up around rivers or lakes and rising waters were well known for their destructive force – even whole cemeteries could be washed away. Emil once had the misfortune of witnessing the grisly detritus being removed from a storm drain. It wasn't exactly a joy for the workers who had to do it either – how they withstood not only recovering but untangling the putrid mess of bones and still rotting corpses was beyond him.

Emil pursued his line of questioning or more accurately, clarification. 'Is one of her sons missing?'

'Maria had seven brothers – septuplets to be precise, but only six of them have been found.'

Emil sighed at what was starting to become a farce. 'Father, the cemetery is only just outside and the valley below at least a mile away so the torrent of water could easily have carried the body down to it. Some farmer will probably find the remains when the fields are ploughed in the spring.'

'They weren't interred in the cemetery and the water only disturbed the shallow topsoil that covered them.' He placed a hand on one of the coffins. 'Maria discovered their remains in the grounds of the house, and one of them is missing.'

CHAPTER FIVE

Emil looked at the coffins. Maria's brothers had almost certainly been murdered – the discovery of a shallow mass grave all but proved it, but by whose hand and why?

He studied one of the caskets. The small wooden box had been hastily constructed with gaps and knotholes visible all over. He bent down and peered into one of them. The burning wick of an altar candle could be seen right through on the other side.

'Padre? When we were in the cellar, you referred to the boys' bodies as *remains*. What exactly is in these coffins?'

'Their bones.' The padre made it sound obvious. 'They have been in the ground for eleven years.'

That surprised Emil, but made sense considering the age and state of what was in the basement.

He recalled what he'd seen so far: the children, the specimen jars and the chair with the strange head-cage device attached. He stood back. 'I'm afraid I'm going to have to look inside each of them.'

The reverend made his way to where he'd placed the truck battery. He may have been God's representative and in charge of his house, but the legal obligations of a mortal man still held sway. He returned with a claw hammer and handed it over. 'Just remember where you are.' Emil was left to the grisly task.

The heel of the tool was inserted under one of the lids and the four nails holding it down gave way. The box contained a hessian sack secured at one end with twine. The size and shape told Emil it contained what he was expecting and he untied it. The sack gave off a strange, oily odour as he did.

The end of a paper refuse bag was revealed, but it was wet with the contents and tore when opened. Emil screwed his face up at the mud-encrusted arm or leg bone that emerged.

The light of the candles meant detail couldn't be seen, but its length in comparison to the coffin made one thing clear – the boy wasn't a toddler. Maybe as old as eight or even ten. A pathologist would be able to determine that through photographs and of the skull in particular. Gritting his teeth, Emil reached inside and searched for it but became frustrated when the familiar shape didn't come to hand. He reluctantly emptied the mess of mud and remains into the coffin. He then realised what the smell was – diesel fuel.

To begin with Emil thought the skull was missing with just the lower jaw present. He wiped away mud in preparation of the pictures, but then noticed it had suffered some kind of blunt-force trauma – all the teeth bar one had been removed and with such force that much of the supporting bone had given way too. Emil was in the process of placing it next to what he now realised was a thigh bone when he spotted the front of the skull.

Expecting the cranium to be behind, Emil prised it from the surrounding earth only to discover why he'd failed to identify the head in the first place – there wasn't one. Just the front of the skull with the upper jaw again showing signs of a determined effort to ensure any existing dental records couldn't be used to identify the child.

Emil wiped as much earth away as he could and grabbed his torch for a better view. Whoever had done this didn't only want to ensure identity would never be known, but what had been done surgically kept a secret too – the precisely drilled incisions the detective was expecting to see appeared impossible to confirm as the cranium had been destroyed in the same brutal way. Emil ran a finger over the sharp edges of what had survived before turning back to the pitiful debris of earth and skeleton that had once been a little boy.

It took a while, but fragments of the crown did eventually reveal themselves. Emil put each one next to the other remains he'd cleaned and kept going – he wanted to see how skilful the surgeon had become before departing the scene of his crime. The detective allowed himself a moment of satisfaction when what he was searching for, appeared.

The shard didn't show a complete hole, but it was enough. Emil took out his handkerchief and with the help of some spit, eked out the semi-circular evidence. He wiped his hands as best he could and retrieved a camera from the holdall.

The sombre organ recital restarted and the padre

made his way back. He drew a sign of the cross on his chest when he saw what Emil had done.

'So, have you finally decided to accept the inevitable end of our mortal selves, Sergeant?'

Emil attached a macro lens to the camera and zoomed in tight on where he thought the pathologist would be most interested. 'Well, I'll tell you what I've found so far, Father and let you decide.'

Emil continued to gather his evidence while explaining the facts. 'The specimens in the basement have undergone some kind of pre or postnatal brain operation that appears to have affected their growth. The children still alive seem to have suffered the same and now we have the bones of six boys found in a shallow grave in the grounds of where your so-called *miracle* took place.'

He put down the camera and picked up the drilled fragment. 'This bears the same evidence, and I'm willing to bet the other remains will too.' Emil regarded the pastor as if to judge him. 'And just in case what happened in Ariloch eleven years ago still isn't clear to you, the skull was deliberately smashed to try and hide the perpetrator's handiwork and a smell of diesel tells me the bodies were probably burned for the same reason.'

Emil provoked him. 'So what do *you* think, Father? Try to help me understand why *Jesus* decided he not only had the divine right to terminate the lives of unborn babies but the existence of six healthy little boys too?'

The padre was unmoved. 'Ashes to ashes, dust to dust, Sergeant. They are all with our Lord God in

Heaven now which is how it should be.' He approached the altar and knelt down to pray.

Emil lost his temper. 'Now listen to me, Padre. The only reason I don't arrest you right now is because I don't believe you're capable of killing anybody let alone these boys, but I'm not stupid.' He pulled the preacher's hands apart. 'Who are you protecting and why?'

The priest wrestled away and stood up. 'To paraphrase something not in the good book, *there are more things in Heaven and earth, and you and I cannot possibly hope to understand them.*' His spit flew. 'Did Noah question why the Ark had to be built or Abraham the need to move his family to Canaan?' Martin prodded his lost sheep in the chest. 'You have much to learn, Emil – even Moses who'd led an entire nation out of slavery found the door to the Promised Land barred to him and all because he dared to question the word of God.' A quote from Isaiah followed, *'Behold, the day of the Lord comes, cruel, with wrath and fierce anger, to make the land a desolation and to destroy its sinners from it.'*

A series of similar passages from the Old Testament were then reeled off as if to prove something, but Emil didn't hear them. He was thinking about two other people who would have been around at the time of the murders and one in particular. His fledgling feelings for her were starting to cloud his judgment.

Emil needed a distraction and anyway, the discovery of the boys' remains and their connection with someone long since departed was above his pay grade now. It was time to pass the whole sorry affair up the chain.

The priest was in the middle of *fire and brimstone* when Emil interrupted him. 'Where's the telephone, Padre?' The still angry host didn't halt his diatribe but did point to the rear of the church.

Emil entered the office, grabbed the receiver and asked the operator for a connection to his precinct. Gomez snatched the phone away from whoever had answered. He was his usual mix of brusque, no-nonsense authority and sarcasm he liked to think was a sense of humour.

'Have you done as instructed, Sergeant? Or am I going to have to redistribute your bonus to a good cause elsewhere?' Laughter in the background just seemed to encourage Emil's boss. Gomez eventually allowed him to speak.

Emil was just getting into the sickening works of the village's very own *Doctor Moreau* when to his disappointment, the inspector announced some difficulty with the line and he would have to call him back. Gomez then put his phone down. Emil thought he heard another receiver being replaced just before doing the same at his end.

The only phone for miles rang as expected and Emil's natural suspicions were confirmed when he heard the unmistakable sound of a third telephone receiver being lifted from its cradle. He was about to warn his boss with the appropriate code word when it became clear the only thing Emil would be required to say during the one-sided conversation was, 'Yes, Sir' at the end of it.

'Now, listen to me, Sergeant. I gave you strict

instructions to ensure everything is buried. I don't give a fuck if it's one, six or six hundred bodies, you're to ensure *all* of them and *all their belongings* are buried. Have I made myself clear?'

CHAPTER SIX

Emil put down the receiver, and tried to come to terms with what he was required to do. Surely that didn't include the orphans? No, of course not – by 'bodies' Inspector Gomez meant those no longer living, but he didn't just mean the remains of the brothers – it was clear the victims in the basement had to be interred too.

'Belongings' didn't require much imagination either – everything connected had to go, but why? Emil was basically being told to dispose of evidence against a murderer. The inspector's integrity as a policeman might have been as grubby as Emil's own, but no detective in his right mind would turn down the chance of bringing someone so monstrous to justice. Unless…

The padre came into the office. 'It's getting late. You need to finish whatever it is you're doing.'

Emil stood up. 'I have what's required, Padre, and will put everything back as found, but there's something I need to check in the house first. Is the generator still running?'

The reverend nodded before looking at the six coffins and the undignified state of one in particular. 'I'll finish up here. You do what you have to.' He turned back to the officer. 'I took each one of them out of the ground with my bare hands, anyway.'

Emil's opinion of the padre mellowed at the thought of what that must have entailed.

Grabbing his bag, Emil walked out of the church and began making his way back up to the house. The campfire had died down, but there was enough of a glow for him to see Maria had joined the children still sitting around it. The boisterous antics of before had been replaced by what looked to be rapt attention of a bedtime story. He decided to stop and listen to Maria's words and soon became just as captivated. *'She would make a wonderful mother,'* he thought to himself.

Emil didn't intend to but found himself sitting on a log next to her just as the final words of the fairy tale were read out.

'... And the prince and the princess lived happily ever after.'

Maria and Emil stared at each other and the children giggled. Emil started to say something genuine for a change when a certain little girl put what was in her hand between them.

Maria's eyes widened at Emil as if any honourable intentions he had towards her rested on his very next decision. He smiled at the child before finally accepting the packet. The little girl grinned back and clasped her hands together in keen anticipation. All the children did.

Aware the jury might still be out, Emil unwound the packet and tipped as little of the crushed biscuit as he could into the palm of his hand. He made sure the child saw him pop the crumbs he selected into his mouth before giving the majority of the treat back to her. She whooped with joy, performed a little victory dance and then hugged them both before running off. Her pleasure affected him.

'I can't get over how happy and well-behaved the children are.'

'We have Uncle Joe to thank for that.'

Emil regarded Maria as if she were as mad as the padre appeared to be. 'How can you say that? He placed a hand on her arm. 'Maria, you do know your brothers were murdered?'

She sobbed. The children fretted as if waiting for Emil to do the right thing. They relaxed again as his arm went around her waist. Maria dropped her head to his shoulder and the youngsters regained their smiles too.

'I don't understand it. He was always so kind and generous to us all.' Maria tilted her head up. 'Why would he do something so awful?'

Emil didn't know if it was the tears or the close proximity of her lips, but it just seemed natural to place his against them, so he did.

The children erupted into a frenzy of joy and began smothering the new love birds with kisses of their own. It took a good few minutes for the adults to calm them and it ended in groans for some as Maria announced it was way past their bedtime. She took hold of two tiny hands and the rest followed behind. She hesitated after a few steps and turned back to her new love interest.

'Are you going back up to the house?' Emil nodded.

'Mama's asleep in one of the bedrooms.' She gave him another one of her looks. 'Don't wake her.'

'I only need to go into the study, anyway.'

Maria appeared to think for a second. 'You won't find anything.' She herded her kittens and they continued on their way. Emil surveyed the retreating scene and wondered if Maria and he would have children of their own one day.

He picked up his bag and a few minutes later, opened the front door to the house. The lights were still on and the reassuring hum of the generator could be heard in the background.

Turning left from the hallway, Emil found the study. It was just as elegant and clean as the rest of the house above ground and doubled as a library. As could be expected, the books that lined the walls contained surgical or medical text with what he presumed to be some of the owner's own handwritten and sketched manuscripts amongst them. The detective couldn't hope to understand what it all meant, but it was plain some serious research and development had gone into whatever the murderer was trying to achieve – or had achieved.

In searching for the identity of the killer, Emil found the drawings dealing with the design and operation of the head-cage device, but it was a strange cradle to grave depiction that intrigued him most. No wonder Padre Martin was convinced of a Second Coming – the hand-drawn graphics appeared to show some kind of provable link between man and God. What had been done to the specimens and the children was detailed too, along with an explanation of the science behind a method of *visiting* Heaven. There was even a Raphael-like depiction of the divine creator at the top of each page.

Emil was starting to understand how a devout man like the padre could be taken in by it all. It must have come as quite a shock when the brothers' remains were found and in such an irreverent state – certainly out of context with what Emil was looking at now. Not that the specimens in the basement were much better off, but they hadn't been baptised which in the eyes of the Church made them little more than pickled eggs.

But that was all academic now. He had his instructions and would carry them out to the letter – as soon as his curiosity of the author's identity had been satisfied. He opened one of the drawers to the desk. It was empty. He tried another. That was empty too. Emil went through the rest but other than the occasional item of stationery they were all void. He tackled a filing cabinet of medical records next, but that proved just as fruitless. Emil was about to start on the rest of the books when he heard a noise behind him. He instinctively took out his pistol.

'Is this what you're looking for?' Maria held out a small booklet.

Emil put the gun away and took the passport from her which he soon realised would never allow international passage, even if it were still in date. The front cover confirmed what he had begun to suspect but refused to believe the moment he saw what was in the basement. Emil opened the official document and stared at the bearer's picture. He'd seen it many times. He checked the name. Emil had seen and heard that many times, too.

The police were already looking for the notorious Nazi – as was the rest of the world.

CHAPTER SEVEN

'You do know who this is and what it probably means?'

Maria nodded. She looked guilty, even though there was no need. 'Are you going to arrest me?'

Emil shook his head. 'It's all now well beyond what I was sent here to do. I have new orders and they don't involve taking anyone into custody.' He picked up some of the anthropological-like sketches the doctor had left behind. 'What I don't understand is why he wanted all of this preserving? Having said that, there's enough evidence in his own country to send him to the gallows.'

Maria took one of the drawings from Emil. 'He didn't. He left strict instructions for it to be destroyed if he didn't return within a month. It was the Church that ordered it to be kept ready, regardless.' She pointed at the sophisticated graphics. 'You can see why. Uncle Joe was close to finding a way to not just go to Heaven but return from it too. I think the Church hoped proof of the hereafter could be used to restore faith in those who'd lost or didn't have it in the first place.'

Emil peered at her. 'And you believe that nonsense?'

'I did when I was younger, but not now. Not now

I've seen what he did to my brothers.' She put her head down and Emil stood up to comfort her.

'It's okay. Everything's okay. We'll find the monster and bring him to justice, I promise you.' The detective may have had a good handle on the law's priorities, but he still had a lot to learn when it came to understanding women's. Maria pushed him away.

'I don't give a damn whether you find him or not – I want my brother back! What are you going to do about it?' Their new relationship appeared to have settled into a familiar routine already.

Emil's shoulders sagged. He knew there was about as much chance of finding her sibling as he had of making chief of police. Same old story. No money and even fewer resources, not to mention the luck required to secure what would undoubtedly result in a seventh coffin anyway. He cared enough about Maria to show willing, though. 'Do you have a photograph?'

Maria reached into her apron and pulled out a family portrait. Although over a decade had passed since it was taken, she and her mother stood out from it, but not so much the septuplets. Their father was absent and a ragged edge to one side indicated he'd probably been torn from it. *Guess I might not have to ask for permission to marry her, then*, Emil said to himself.

He was about to enquire after her father when something about the brothers made Emil pursue a different question. 'How old are you in this picture, Maria?'

'Fourteen.'

Emil switched on a desk lamp and retrieved the magnifying glass he'd seen in one of the drawers earlier.

The photograph was a professional studio portrait, but its underdeveloped nature told him it was probably one of the trial and error prints made prior to the final copy. The washed-out appearance meant much of the detail had been lost, but one thing was evident – the boys were the same height as their sister.

Emil thought the remains he'd studied in the church might have made the boy as much as ten, but a teenager? He passed the magnifying glass over the memento in the hope of solving the mystery when a framed version of the exact same image was placed in front of him. Maria's mother stood back and folded her arms.

It was the final print approved and the clearer detail lead Emil to an unexpected revelation.

The reason why Maria and her mother could be made out in the first picture was because of their skin and hair. Along with the man still attached to this particular version of the scene, both were much darker than the boys. No wonder the septuplets could barely be made out in Maria's copy – they were white with blond hair. There was no doubt in Emil's mind, had the print been in colour their eyes would probably have been blue.

Maria's mother's roots were Pampas and her father's southern European, but the boys' own origins lay well north of both continents – maybe even as far as Scandinavia. It would explain why they were so tall for their age. Emil concluded they had been adopted.

Mrs Fierro must have seen the policeman's

judgmental look many times before – she turned on him. 'I carried my boys for nine months and nearly died giving birth to them!'

Maria came to her mother's defence. 'It's true. I was only eight, but I can remember Uncle Joe delivering them like it was yesterday.'

Emil started to fear for his own sanity. 'Eight? That makes the boys *six* in this picture!' They were only a few inches shorter than the man in it.

The septuplets weren't just identical – their growth and angelic appearance were unusual too. They couldn't have been more opposite to the children Emil had seen so far – alive or otherwise.

The picture that had begun developing in the detective's mind ever since he first set foot in Ariloch began revealing its details too. Emil went through the evil eugenicist's manuscripts again. 'Mrs Fierro. May I ask how you became pregnant with the boys?'

'It's called, in vitro fertilisation.' The three of them jumped at the padre's sudden appearance. Maria's mother went to him and he put his arm around her. Martin used his free hand to pick up one of the sketches. 'Uncle Joe really was the saviour of this village you know. He arrived here not long after the end of the war when the people were desperate for relief from a conflict of their own – against nature.'

The padre pulled up a chair and sat Maria's mother down. 'There are only so many crop failures and livestock diseases a community can withstand before it gives up all hope and Uncle Joe arrived with the one thing everyone including the Church needed – money. Each time God saw fit to punish the people for their sins, Uncle Joe brought in fresh stock and told the villagers they'd been forgiven. Throw in the blessing of healing the sick and you can see why the village would do anything for him.' The implication of the padre's next statement didn't appear to concern him in the least. 'Including the offering of women and children for his work.' He passed Emil a sketch detailing the process required to impregnate a surrogate mother with pre-fertilised ovum.

Like the other drawings, it too had a depiction of the Holy Father at the top that implied it came with some kind of divine approval. The reverend echoed that sentiment. 'God's work.'

The picture in Emil's mind became complete. The Nazi eugenicist hadn't just continued his evil experiments after escaping what should have been his fate in Germany – he'd finished them in this tiny South American village some twenty years later and by using its people as human guinea pigs. Lab rats needed to refine what the monster had always planned for the embryos he brought with him. Even six of those were callously murdered once the job was done – the creation of just one *perfect* child. A boy.

A boy the notorious doctor took with him when he left.

CHAPTER EIGHT

Emil lit a cigarette. 'I'm sorry, but I've been given strict instructions to destroy all of this.' The three of them looked at each other before nodding in unison.

Emil was concerned the pastor's somewhat misguided commitment to God might interfere with the process. 'You do understand that means *everything*, Padre?'

'Yes, I understand. I received a telephone call instructing me to assist you.'

'Telephone call? Did my inspector speak to you, too?'

'No, the bishop.'

Emil had suspected a higher organisation lay behind Gomez's almost desperate demands for the evidence to be destroyed and assumed it to be the government when he saw the passport, but the Church's involvement and in such a rapid way implied a level of national interest bordering on the hysterical.

Emil needed to test his host's apparent change of heart. 'Padre, will you help me carry these manuscripts down to the campfire?'

The pastor seemed preoccupied but otherwise willing enough. 'Yes, of course.'

The detective extinguished the Marlboro and the four of them gathered as many of the documents as they could. Emil kept an eye on the priest as they descended the hill. He was compliant but plainly troubled by whatever the bishop had said.

They reached the deserted campfire and soon had the paperwork reduced to ash. The man of God made no complaint or excuse throughout so Emil assumed he would still be on board when it came to executing the main part of the plan – burning the house to the ground. Emil put it to him there and then.

There appeared to be no issues with that either. A full moon silhouetted the cross on the church and the padre stared at it while making a suggestion. 'It might be best to do it straight after the funerals tomorrow. You'll need somewhere to sleep tonight anyway.' They all agreed.

The bed was comfortable, but Emil was plagued by nightmares.

The infamous doctor and his unspeakable experiments featured, and animated visions of the most grotesque tormented Emil throughout. Although every imaginable horror was presented, the twisted surgeon's figment also appeared to taunt with some kind of purgatory that lay in wait for those deemed less worthy of his attention.

Emil feared what the madman would do if Maria made an appearance and when she did, tried everything he could to protect her – all to no avail of course. But then something unsettling as it was horrifying happened.

Instead of being just as fearful, Emil's new love seized the doctor with both hands and forced him into the chair instead. The look on the twisted medic's face indicated it was the last thing he was expecting, but it was Maria's expression that shocked Emil more as she then rammed the head-cage down, picked up an electric drill and began boring into the doctor's skull.

Emil could see this was no mere act of revenge – she was enjoying the experience and the maniacal expression she maintained throughout told the young policeman he was going to be next. Sure enough, once everything Maria needed from the doctor's brain had been removed, the body was unceremoniously tipped into a vat of formaldehyde. The scene was so vivid, Emil thought he could smell its pungent odour.

As anticipated, Maria reached for him next and, despite his love for her, Emil fought against the vision as if his life depended on it.

'Get up, Emil!'

There was no way Emil was getting into that chair and he thrashed his arms as Maria took a firm hold. Her mother appeared and grabbed him too.

'Emil, wake up!'

His body was being shaken by the force of their combined strength.

'Emil, wake up – Father Martin's in the basement!'

He sat bolt upright. The smell of embalming fluid in the air was unmistakable. Both women were upset but of the two, Maria's mother the most hysterical.

'He said he had to baptise the children and I thought

he meant those in the village, but that can't be right because they've already been—'

Emil cut her off as his half-awake mind realised the seriousness of the situation. He shot out of bed, ran downstairs in his underwear and began choking on the fumes. He shouted back upstairs for them to grab their things and get out of the house as soon as possible. Emil burst into the kitchen – the door to the basement was open.

'Padre Martin, get the hell out of there!' No answer.

A sound of breaking glass made Emil grab a cloth to cover his face.

Halfway down the steps, the pastor could be seen – shattering every one of the doctor's macabre collection with a hammer. The contents then received a prayer and a sprinkle of holy water from a flask. The putrid mess that slopped across the floor made the atmosphere almost impossible to bear.

Emil dropped the cloth from his face. 'Padre, you *must* get out. The fumes are highly flammable. The slightest spark and the place will go up like a bomb!'

The pastor stopped. 'Isn't that what you want?' He stared at the sea of dead and decaying flesh. 'Isn't this what *God* wants?' He returned to the containers still intact on the shelves. 'Get yourself and the women away from here, Sergeant Vazquez.'

Emil put the cloth back to his face and took a deep breath through the material. He ran down the last few steps, determined to do whatever it took to get the reverend away from certain danger. The last jar was broken, the remaining contents of the flask emptied, and the final Hail Mary uttered just as Emil reached the bottom. The padre took out a box of matches and Emil stopped. The drawer to it was slid open.

'This is all my fault. I stood back, let the Devil wreak havoc and did nothing.' The padre looked at the stunned policeman. 'Pray for me, my friend.' He took out a match and struck it.

The basement had no windows or other doors, so the only release for the pressure wave created by the blast was back up the steps. It took Emil with it. He shot out at the top, across the kitchen floor and clouted his head against the wall at the far end. The searing heat on his skin dissipated as the initial blast was sucked back by the vacuum created, but a dazed Emil then watched in horror as flames began spreading out from the basement once more. A plentiful supply of formaldehyde vapour encouraged the consumption of everything that lay in its path.

Emil shook his head and tried to stand, but increasing heat forced him to stay crouched. He found the door and scrambled through both it and the rest of the house as fast as he could, lungs desperate for fresh air. The failed rescuer reached the front door just as the flames caught up with him and they assisted Emil's escape by ejecting him out of the house like the unwanted guest he was.

Emil staggered down the path where Maria and her mother helped pull him to safety. They and the children then began a series of half-hugs and inspections to ensure he was still intact.

It took a couple of minutes for Emil to realise how lucky he'd been and then, like the rest, he turned to watch the house burn down; a funeral pyre for those forgotten by God but remembered by Father Martin.

CHAPTER NINE

They stood in silence beside the graves. No one knew what to say.

Padre Martin had done what was required – the dead and all their belongings were now buried.

Emil's eyes wandered over the rest of the graveyard. Despite the village having so few inhabitants, it was unsettling to see the brothers weren't the only children recently interred. Juvenile funerals were a regular feature judging by the many areas of disturbed earth and the unweathered wooden crosses that marked them. There were even some freshly dug graves and their size made it plain they weren't intended for adults. Earth lay piled to one side as if ready to be shovelled back in at a moment's notice.

Maria's mother broke the silence. 'They need flowers.' Some of the children took that as an instruction and headed off with her into the woods to find some. Emil noticed his little stalker wasn't amongst them. He glanced around. She didn't seem to be anywhere.

The object of his affections looked at the smoke rising from the top of the hill. 'What will you do now?'

'Head back to the city I suppose.' He took her

hand. 'What about you?' He paused before adding, 'Us.'

Maria ran her fingers through his. 'Do you really think a relationship between a city boy like you and a country girl like me could work?'

She made it sound romantic, but Emil knew what she meant. Their two worlds weren't just distant geographically; they were poles apart culturally too. His new love may have been part Spanish, but that still made her an *indio* to some and even though his southern European heritage was just as 'corrupt' with North African ancestry, their visible difference wouldn't go unnoticed and especially in the country's capital – racism was as endemic in Argentina as corruption in its police. Emil knew being a third-generation immigrant from the wrong part of the world meant he would never make chief of police but by marrying Maria he could say goodbye to inspector too.

He dismissed the fears. 'We'll make it work. I'll find a way.'

Maria made it obvious she wanted to kiss him and he bent down to oblige. She studied his face afterwards. 'I've decided naivety is your most attractive feature.'

Emil narrowed his lips and was about to protest when a hand was placed over his mouth. 'I have to be here for the children. Write to me at the hospital and don't be a stranger.'

Emil wanted their relationship to mean a lot more than that and was about to explain it when shouting made them look up.

'Maria! Senor! Come quick!' It was Pedro. They ran to him.

He was standing next to one of the dwellings that appeared to double as animal shelters. As if to emphasise that, a couple of chickens shot out when Emil and Maria stooped to enter it.

The interior of the accommodation couldn't have been more opposite to what Emil was expecting and it surprised him. The open space was laid out like any other child's bedroom – only it was the tidiest he'd seen. Clean and well organised, the few toys it contained were placed more like trophies than forms of entertainment. A hessian mat lay in the middle of a swept floor and a tiny child-sized wooden chair sat next to an equally small table which held a cardboard dolls' house that had seen better days. It was arranged as if to show off to any visitor how its owner hoped to live one day. Emil turned his attention to her.

Curled up like a foetus, the little girl lay motionless in her cot-like bed. Emil placed the back of his hand against her cheek. It was cold. Tiny hands could be seen above the blanket that covered her and Emil began weeping the moment he saw what was still in them.

From initial pity on arrival to growing disquiet with his investigation, to the horror of the basement, to his utter disbelief at the final exposure of the truth, all the emotions Emil had thus far managed to suppress came tumbling forth at the sight of an empty cellophane wrapper. He fell to his knees.

'I didn't even know your name.' The thoughtless

oversight seemed to complete his feelings of hopeless inadequacy.

Maria was just as moved, but the almost weekly occurrence made her better able to cope with yet another premature end to an innocent life. She drew a sign of the cross before putting a hand on Emil's shoulder. 'Her name was Sofia.'

Emil took out a handkerchief to dry his tears but ended up wiping them away from Sofia's tiny misshapen head instead.

He regained his composure and wrapped the blanket around her.

'I'm going to find your brother, Maria.' Emil lifted Sofia's body from the bed. 'And the monster that did this. And when I do, I'm going to kill him.'

CHAPTER TEN

Emil drifted back down the track. He couldn't remember a time when he'd felt so dejected. Other than meeting the girl of his dreams, there wasn't one single positive aspect of his visit to Ariloch. Even Maria's reciprocated feelings were tempered by a frustrating but admirable duty towards the orphans, not to mention her 'cultural' concerns.

She was right of course. If their relationship were to survive, it would need to be conducted away from his judgmental boss and colleagues, but that meant a visit whenever he had leave and three days of that would be spent travelling. What serious relationship survives on being together just a couple of weeks a year? Emil didn't know but he sure as hell was going to give it a try.

He choked at the thought of Sofia. Without a padre, he couldn't even attend her funeral. The best he could manage was the construction of a wooden box within which he laid her body along with some of her toys. Emil left the wrapper in her hands. It didn't seem right to remove it somehow. Maria had ensured the Church was made aware of what had happened and a new padre would be sent but in the meantime, she and her mother would attend a vigil of the little girl's coffin – along with the remaining orphans' needs. Emil wondered how long it would take for all the children to succumb to the evil they'd suffered.

His heart sank further at the pointlessness of it all. Even the telephone call he'd made to the inspector just before leaving couldn't snap him out of it. Gomez had appeared pleased enough, but the concern he expressed for his sergeant's safe return was a little over the top, even for him: 'Be careful when you're on your own, Emil. Be *very* careful.'

Emil stopped. Having travelled up just the day before, he knew how exposed the track was and anyone seeing him would have known a return journey all but inevitable. He put down his bag and took out a map to see if there was an alternative route.

He'd only just opened it when behind him came the sound of footsteps. Emil took out his gun but then let out a sigh of relief when he saw who it was. As ever, Pedro's eyes darted back and forth between the Browning and its owner.

Emil was about to put the pistol away when it hit him – the chance to salvage something *positive* from his visit.

Had anyone from the Church been present they would have no doubt disapproved of the idea – along with Maria and her mother – but if anything, that would make the moment that much sweeter. Emil didn't care if handing back fewer rounds of ammunition than signed for would cause questions and he certainly didn't care if his boss found out. No, Emil was going to make one mischievously curious orphan's day – maybe even his life; Emil was going to let Pedro fire a gun.

The rusting carcass of an old car lay nearby. The policeman cocked his pistol, released the safety and put a bullet through the windshield. Pedro's mouth dropped open at the shock of both cartridge and glass exploding. The smoking weapon was then offered and the way Pedro ran towards it made Emil feel better already, but he wasn't stupid – the gun was hoisted out of reach and a pair of handcuffs presented instead. If anything, the teenager appeared more excited at the prospect of being 'arrested'.

Pedro grinned and lifted his withered arm. Emil secured his own wrist first and then his eager pupil's. There would be no repeat of what had happened the day before.

Keeping the pistol pointing towards the old Ford, the boy's just as enthusiastic instructor encouraged him to take a firm hold of the grip. Pedro wrapped his hand around it – that was all the opportunity he needed.

Within less than a second, the gun had not only been snatched away from Emil yet again but the handcuffs slipped too. The stunned policeman prepared to pursue another fruitless chase when to his sickening horror, Pedro stood his ground and pointed the gun – straight at Emil's chest.

Had Emil had time to think, he maybe would have pondered his murder as a fitting end to an investigation that seemed to consist of nothing but death. Even the style of it would be appropriate – his killer, with probably less than a year to live and nothing to live for, would, at least, be able to challenge St Peter with something, anything to avenge the evil of what had been done to him. What had been done to him and all the other children by a seemingly kindly man from a land far away.

Emil closed his eyes and tried not to blame anyone, but himself. Not even his boss. A boss who had warned him to be extra vigilant just an hour earlier. Emil never thought he'd make inspector anyway. He whispered goodbye to Maria just as two shots rang out.

He opened his eyes to see what Death looked like. Pedro lowered the gun. Something made Emil spin round. It was the final breaths of two men who now lay dead on the ground.

Emil searched his thumping chest as if expecting to find holes in it, but the position of the bodies indicated the two projectiles had passed harmlessly either side of him. Pedro crept up, as if not knowing if what he'd done was a good or a bad thing. Emil retrieved his gun before making sure the boy knew it was most definitely the former – the weapons still in the hands of the would-be assassins attested to that.

Pedro was beside himself with joy. It was as if he had finally done something that didn't result in a hiding, humiliation or exclusion. Something that ended in what he'd always wanted but never received – a hug. Like Sofia the night before, he whooped and performed a dance which ended in a hug for Emil too and then a run back to the village as fast as his little legs could carry him; to tell the rest of the children no doubt. Not that they would believe him. Emil didn't think they would swallow his version of events back at the station either. Pulse still well above normal, the policeman put himself back on duty and approached the bodies as any other homicide officer would.

The shot through the windscreen of the Ford must have made them break cover from their ambush. It was clearly a put-up job. Light clothing and stylish leather jackets meant they weren't part of some rag-tag communist militia prepared to lie in wait for days on the off-chance – these were professional hit men.

Emil didn't expect to find any identification but was about to search them anyway when he recognised the type of weapon each had planned to kill him with – a standard police-issue Browning nine-millimetre. The temperature of the air appeared to plummet and Emil shivered. He reached inside each jacket hoping not to find what he did – their warrant cards.

His eyes wandered back up the track. The executioner could still be seen, running. Pedro turned and waved. Emil was in shock but he waved back. The loose end of the handcuffs dangled in front of his eyes and he examined them to see how the slippery eel had managed to escape so easily.

It was quite simple really. Pedro used his good hand to tear through the high-tensile steel.

CHAPTER ELEVEN

Inspector Gomez opened the door to his office and switched on the light. He had stared down enough gun barrels in his career not to be too fazed by what was being pointed at him. The sight of a sergeant sitting at his desk was a different matter, however.

'Get the fuck out of my chair.'

'Give me one good reason why I shouldn't kill you right now.'

Thirty years of dealing with desperate men holding guns told the seasoned officer his dishevelled junior was serious, but Gomez still thought it worth giving seniority one last try.

'I said, get the fuck out of my chair before I walk over there, take that pistol out of your hand and beat some sense into you with it.' Gomez wondered when the duty desk officer would notice his raised voice. It shouldn't be long – it was six in the morning and the place was as quiet as the grave.

Emil stood up and extended his aim. He threw what he had in his other hand onto the desk. 'Why did you send them to kill me?'

The inspector didn't need to look at what was in

front of him. The bodies of the policemen had been found two days earlier. He regarded Emil in a way he never thought he would. 'Did you kill them?'

'No. The person who released themselves from these did it.' He threw the useless handcuffs on top of the warrant cards. 'But my own people want me dead and I want to know why.'

The tension in the older man eased at the relief his sergeant wasn't a cop-killer but also because the query implied at least a chance of surviving the current encounter. Gomez looked at the rent and twisted metal. Where the hell was that idiot of a desk officer?

'I didn't send them. I was told to ensure any bodies found in Ariloch were buried – that's all. I assumed some criminal gang with connections had paid to have their tracks covered.'

Emil lowered his gun a little. 'Who told you?'

Gomez glanced over his shoulder as music from the local radio station began playing. The desk officer was in for the beating of his life – assuming his boss still had his to dish it out, of course. Gomez refocused back on Emil. 'I receive my orders in the same way you do – the next rank up.'

Emil sat back down and motioned for his superior to do the same. He kept the Browning pointing at Gomez. 'If you didn't send them, then whoever was listening in on our telephone conversations, did.'

Gomez was determined to try and exert some kind of control over the situation. 'Do you think I don't know that? The second you opened your mouth about the basement, I knew two things: what I'd sent you to do was much more than a routine cover-up job and your life was in great danger and not from some Marxist gang.' He picked up what was left of the handcuffs and studied them. 'Whatever's going on is well above our pay grade – why the hell do you think I told you to watch your back?' The gun was lowered a little more.

Emil reached inside his jacket and took out a photocopy of a passport. He passed it to Gomez.

Like his junior, discovering what was in the basement had made Gomez realise that one of the world's most wanted men was probably the man responsible. Seeing his official picture just confirmed it.

'Where's the original?'

'Somewhere safe. I want you to tell the captain that if anything untoward should happen to me, you or anyone else then it will immediately be made public.' Emil applied the gun's safety, turned it around and offered it to his boss. Gomez took it. 'And that includes the paperwork detailing the involvement of Church and state. I shouldn't think the world would be very impressed to discover this country not only supported but continues to protect the Nazi to this day.'

It was all nonsense of course. The passport was certainly safe but not in the hands of anyone with connections to a *free* press – that was just as sewn-up by the junta as everything else. The evil doctor's manuscripts didn't exist anymore either. No, Emil was trying to protect his life and that of anyone he knew with the bluff of the century. It didn't impress his boss who hit him as hard as he could to show it.

'Now get the fuck out of my office!'

Emil dragged himself up from the floor and put a hand to his chin. It was wet. Gomez stood to one side and followed him out. He walked over to the duty officer, struck him in the face too, picked up the radio and ended *Baker Street* by smashing it to the floor.

'Just in case anyone else is in doubt as to who's in charge around here.'

Gomez returned to his office but paused on the way to slam Emil's gun down in front of him.

'And the next time you decide to take on the big boys I suggest you look in your desk first to see if your boss hasn't already second-guessed what his idiot of a junior police sergeant probably has planned given he survived one assassination attempt and is desperate not to experience another.' Gomez entered his office and turned around. 'Now go home and get cleaned up – you stink!' The door was slammed shut.

Emil glanced at his gun, the stunned look on the desk corporal's face and then at the blood on his handkerchief. He stemmed the flow with it again and went through his desk.

The first thing Emil saw was the envelope which he assumed contained the bribe payments promised – or rather the 'fair' share expected. Guilt joined physical discomfort when he realised his boss had been true to his word. It amounted to far more than Emil could have achieved on his own. He made himself feel better by assuming it was Gomez's way of assuaging his own guilt at putting him through the whole nightmare in the first place. But then Emil opened the largest drawer.

The packet sealed with brown paper was so thick it couldn't possibly have fitted anywhere else. Emil estimated how much was in it. Gomez, the old fox. He must have realised if you're going to make the bluff of the century then you may as well dress it up for the occasion.

The wad of cash must have contained at least a year's salary and as much as Emil would love to splash out on a new car or holiday, there was still no guarantee he would live long enough to enjoy either. He had to think of his future with Maria, anyway, so took out a pen and began writing her address on it. He then realised part of the packet was torn and needed resealing. The colour of what was exposed made him stop.

He looked up to the front desk. The corporal was still licking his wounds so Emil tore the paper some more.

It confirmed the amount he was expecting but not the currency, which came as a complete surprise – US dollar bills.

1979

CHAPTER TWELVE

The old man leaned on the gate and closed his eyes. He'd only walked a few paces. He didn't look like the perpetrator of some of the world's worst atrocities. Decades on the run from justice would seem to have taken their toll – scant compensation for his evil acts of course. Emil gripped the gun harder.

It had taken two years to find him. A task that had put Emil's own health at risk – Auschwitz's infamous 'Angel of Death' was being protected at every level and although the cost of penetrating that shield had been covered by the 'negotiated' payments, every dollar of it aroused unwanted interest somewhere and staying ahead of that had been crucial – including a distance from his boss. Never mind having to take an assassin's bullet, Gomez would do more than just punch Emil if he knew where he was.

Emil wondered what Maria was doing now. Their love had continued to build and was stronger than ever but seeing each other for just a couple of days each month was beginning to take its toll. He'd looked into getting a transfer, but as much as love conquers all, they both agreed careers should come first. The good news was there would soon be enough money to make a reality of Padre Martin's hopes for her. Institutionalised racism meant Maria having to attend a medical school in the United States but Emil would be immensely proud if she did become a doctor. He tried not to think of what the far greater distance could mean for their relationship.

But there were more immediate concerns and Emil remained as determined as ever to avenge the murder of her brothers and the rest of the orphans. Out of the original thirty-two children, just Pedro remained. The steady supply of money had helped pay for their needs but there was little that could be done medically and even though the new padre did his spiritual best, one by one, the orphans succumbed to the evil doctor's crimes. It was like witnessing some kind of enforced extinction.

Pedro would soon go the same way of course. Even though the boy was now a man, he still appeared no more than ten-years-old and would welcome Emil to the village just as excitedly as the moment he realised he'd saved the policeman's life. But Pedro tired quickly now and his days of being able to bound over brooks and fences like a monkey or pull the trigger of a gun let alone break open a set of handcuffs were long gone. Emil had tried to get him to repeat the feat but even at his fittest, Pedro didn't seem able to understand the question let alone demonstrate it again. Maria said she suspected most of the children had possessed the skill but rarely exercised it and only when stressed – Sofia lifting Emil away from the door to the basement being an example.

But the vile perpetrator was now in front of Emil, and he expected the answer to that and many other questions were about to be revealed. Right before conducting some brain surgery of his own – using an unregistered nine-millimetre pistol.

Once the monster's lair had been found, Emil conducted the operation like any other stake-out and now had enough of the routine understood – the Nazi would pause at his front door to ensure no one had followed before checking again by looking out of the window and then, a few minutes after that, taking a seat in the back yard to smoke a cigarette and read a newspaper. He clearly had no idea what was about to happen to him – his eyes were shut most of the time. Emil couldn't explain it, but he had a strange feeling of being watched whenever that happened.

He opened a map to check his escape route. The former farm was far enough away from its nearest neighbour for screams not to be heard but two or three rounds from the Browning would be a different matter. The remoteness made witnesses unlikely but any person seen running afterwards would attract attention, so no matter what, Emil would force himself to walk the mile or so to where he'd parked the car with the false plates, ditching the gun *en route*. He refolded the map, checked his watch, and headed towards the rear of the building.

The sight and smell of cigarette smoke rising from the backyard reassured him. Emil ducked down behind the wall that surrounded it just as a stomach ache began. He cursed the untimely onset and crept up to the ungated access. He took a chance his quarry would be engrossed in a news item and poked his head through the entrance for a better view. Emil was in luck – not only was the butcher reading his newspaper, but he had it open with both hands, obscuring sight of everything else.

Emil was about to take advantage of this good fortune when without warning, the cramps increased and with such ferocity he had to drop the gun to grab his stomach. If that didn't end any chance of catching his prey unawares, a spontaneous cry of agony must have done. Emil fell to the ground, cursing.

The pain was coming through in waves and in between Emil tried to recover the gun – the level of agony increased. He withdrew his outstretched arm and the cramps reduced. Emil looked to see what advantage his target had taken of the situation but to his amazement, the doctor not only hadn't moved but appeared to be still engrossed in the newspaper!

Pain became discomfort again, and Emil felt well enough to stand. A corner of the newspaper fluttered in the wind but otherwise didn't move. How strange. Emil decided to approach the apparently deaf reader. He pulled the top of the broadsheet down only to realise why the Nazi hadn't responded – he was dead.

Not only dead but just expired. The cigarette in his mouth was still burning, he didn't appear to be breathing and his eyes were closed. Emil felt for a pulse. He couldn't find one but the flesh on the body's arm was still warm. He had quite literally just died. There was no doubt about it, the look on the face was identical to that of the policeman's two would-be-assassins from a couple of years back – devoid of all life.

Emil sat down in a chair opposite, stomach still complaining. Talk about mixed emotions. He felt everything: relief, disappointment, shock. Even a frustrating sense of being cheated out of his form of justice. Emil pondered what to do next.

The door to the kitchen was open so he could try searching the house for the answers he, and what was left of the Fierro family, were after. It was a long shot but there was nothing better to do and certainly no need to rush – even if someone turned up, a lack of bullet holes in the body meant he could probably bluff or bribe his way out. Emil looked at the gun still lying in the dirt as another wave of abdominal agony began. He needed to get rid of that weapon in case it incriminated him. The pain subsided again.

Hot ash from the Marlboro was about to drop onto the newspaper, so Emil removed both from the cadaver's possession, stubbed out the cigarette in an ashtray and folded the broadsheet down next to it. He then lit his own smoke before setting out in the direction of some woods nearby. Pain resumed as soon as the gun was back in his hand but subsided as he walked. Before long, he was out of sight and scraping a hole in the forest floor. Pistol buried, he wandered back.

Emil's thoughts returned to Maria on the way. He had a strange feeling she would be both sad and pleased at the passing of her not-so-favourite uncle, especially without a shot having been fired, but disappointed if her love returned without knowing which one of her brothers had survived. Or if he was even alive. He would be nineteen now if he were – Pedro's age. That would be the only thing they would have in common, though. Emil took out the framed picture Maria's mother had demanded the doctor be tormented with. No chance of that now. Not that a monster like him would have been moved by it. Emil reached the entrance to the yard again and looked up from the portrait. The cigarette fell from his lips. Someone had placed the newspaper back in the body's hands. The joker had even lit it another smoke!

Emil glanced around and instinctively put his hand to where the pistol once was. He was about to run and retrieve it from the woods when the top half of the paper was folded down.

'I'm sorry – I must have fallen asleep. I'm always doing that. Thank you for saving my newspaper, I'm surprised I haven't set fire to myself in the past.'

CHAPTER THIRTEEN

'But, you were *dead*. I checked your pulse.'

'I'm afraid that mistake often gets made with someone so close to dying of old age.' Doctor Mengele smiled. 'Don't worry. You're not the first and certainly not the most qualified to get it wrong – there's been many an embarrassed medic or disappointed pathologist before now.'

The monster finished folding his newspaper and placed it back on the table. 'It wasn't so long ago people were inadvertently being buried alive. Grave robbers often opened coffins bearing evidence of where the occupant had tried clawing their way out. Add the blood that must have been spilled during that to the apparent lengthening of nails and teeth by decomposition and it's easy to see where the vampire myth came from.' Mengele stood up. 'But then we humans have always had difficulty telling fact from fiction.'

Being faced with an evil far greater than Bram Stoker could ever have imagined made Emil make two fists but the return of cramps forced him to grab his stomach again. The pains eased once more. 'I know what a body looks like, Mengele, especially one that died just seconds before and you were dead.' An onset of nausea made Emil sit down.

'Mengele. Now there's a name I haven't heard in a long time. I've used so many aliases since first coming to South America I've lost track of who I really am.' He sat back down next to his visitor. 'I believe you know me as 'Uncle Joe'.'

Emil was still being distracted by discomfort but picked up on what the doctor had said. 'How do you know that?'

'Just a feeling.'

The policeman-turned-vigilante wanted to get on with his questions but the pain refused to go. He put the framed portrait in front of his enemy instead.

Mengele studied it. He placed a hand on the glass and became sad. 'Maria.'

Emil's pain evaporated. He looked at the doctor – he was in tears.

If Emil's emotions had been mixed before, they were completely at odds now. It was like looking at a different person – an old man with a lifetime of regrets that an image had made too much to bear. Maybe that's what it was. Like an empty biscuit wrapper that had once tipped Emil over the edge, maybe a simple photograph was all it took for a monster to see the horror of its actions.

Mengele bowed his head. 'How are Maria and her mother?'

Emil's stomach ache returned. Strange. The doctor's head was scarred – the psychopath had actually operated on himself. 'You'll be pleased to hear they're still suffering from their loss, thanks to you.'

Mengele's lips tightened. 'I'm afraid you won't find me a very apologetic Nazi and if you're looking for an acceptable answer to my actions then you're going to leave disappointed.' He gazed towards the woods. 'Whatever you decide to do.'

Emil couldn't take his hands off his belly. 'I expected you to be completely unrepentant, Mengele, and I'm not here to listen to excuses, but how could anyone carry out such evil?'

'It's all relative, Sergeant. Some people would be just as shocked at your blatant abuse of families desperate to find their loved ones. I wonder what Maria would have to say if she knew the man she intends to marry extorts money from the weak and vulnerable?'

Emil ignored how Mengele could possibly have known that and snapped at him. 'That's completely different. Taking bribes doesn't involve the physical torture and murder of children – don't even think about comparing the two.'

The Nazi didn't let up. 'So the fact many Argentinians turn to suicide or starve to death through the poverty you cause doesn't bother you? And what about *the disappeared* themselves? I suppose your involvement in that particular genocide is just as acceptable.'

Emil lost his temper. 'How the junta runs this country has nothing to do with me; I just do my duty. The fact it results in thousands of deaths is just an unfortunate but sad necessit—' He became quiet.

'You and I are not so different, Sergeant. We *both* did or do our duty. It's only outsiders who fail to understand the necessity of having to kill an entire race of people to make the world a better place. As long as the perpetrators remain capable of writing the history books, nobody would even know let alone care.' He leaned towards the younger man. 'Have you thought about how *you* might have to escape the country of *your birth* should this particular military dictatorship fall?'

Emil stared at the ground. He'd always had a low opinion of his fellow man but thought himself basically good. He now realised he was no different to anybody else. Like beauty, the difference between good and evil appeared to be in the eye of the beholder.

'Of course, there's little difference between your president and the Fuhrer too. Hitler was just as impatient. I and many others often tried to get him to understand the long-term benefits of the carrot as well as the stick but he always chose brawn over brain. He really was the bloodthirsty tyrant the history books paint him to be, you know.'

Emil's physical pain reduced just as his emotional discomfort increased. He got back to the purpose of his mission. 'What were you doing in Ariloch, Mengele?'

The German beamed. 'Continuing my research into the eradication of war.'

CHAPTER FOURTEEN

Emil grabbed him by the lapels. 'Now listen to me, you old fuck. The whole world knows about the horrific experiments you carried out on children at Auschwitz so if you're now saying that was done to end wa—'

Emil suddenly realised he was gripping his *own* neck tightly. The doctor was still sitting a few feet away – his eyes were closed but the position of his hands made it clear what was going on. Emil could only just get the words out. '*Let me go!*'

Involuntary strangulation instantly became a wilful massage. Mengele had put a hand to his own neck as if he too, needed time to recover.

Emil couldn't stop coughing. 'How did you do that?'

It was a while before he got a response, and a fatalistic one at that. 'Go and retrieve your gun, Sergeant. Finish what you came here to do.'

Emil controlled his fit and thought about recovering the pistol. The idea wasn't accompanied by pain. He looked back at the doctor. 'Not before you tell me what you were doing in Ariloch.'

Mengele glared at his would-be assassin. 'What's the

point? You'll only get upset again, and I'd rather not die tired of trying to fight you off.'

The still angry but now intrigued young man would have to control his temper if he were to get the answers he came for. Despite his revulsion, Emil had to listen and learn from everything this man had to say. Mengele had clearly achieved a good deal more than just superhuman strength in Ariloch.

Pedro's handiwork was placed on the table.

Mengele had recovered enough to inspect them. 'Which one of the children did this?' Emil told him.

The doctor put the useless handcuffs back down. He studied the family portrait again before lifting his head towards the fields and woods beyond. 'Why do you think we're here, Sergeant?'

Emil groaned inside. If he were to get what he came for, it looked as if he was going to have to suffer an old man's ramblings first. Emil decided to humour him. 'I don't know – be happy?'

'Ah! Happiness – the ultimate goal which for some reason we spend most of our lives struggling to achieve.' He turned to the frustrated listener. 'Don't you find it interesting that *all* life on this planet spends most of its time struggling?'

Emil didn't bother answering.

'In nature, the struggle for survival is life's only purpose. It has to be. The Earth might be beautiful but it's far from a comfortable place. An uncertain climate, limited food resources and predators alone keep most living things on their toes.' He pointed towards a weed growing through a crack in the paving. 'I could concrete over that plant again and again but it would still try and fight its way to the surface.' A visiting bird tussled with a worm making its own appearance through the hardened cement. 'Wild animals are the same. Everything they do involves struggling to survive and usually just long enough to produce offspring.'

Mengele seemed to think he knew the meaning of life. 'And up until a hundred thousand years ago we were no different. But then along came our ability to make life easier – language, written and then the printed word, the agricultural and industrial revolutions – all of which apparently came with a need to break the human race up from the hunter gatherers we once were into those that understood these new inventions and those that were required to work them.'

He turned his attention back to Emil. 'Which meant the knowledgeable became the masters and the ignorant their slaves.'

Under different circumstances Emil might have found it interesting but he wasn't there to philosophise. 'Get to the point, Mengele.'

'Well, aren't you intrigued to know why man's ability to make life easier is the reason why we go to war in the first place?'

Emil shrugged at what he thought was obvious. 'I guess it's got something to do with all those pissed-off slaves.'

'Actually, far from it. Keeping them under control was the easy bit and still is – just use their ignorance to create a culture of fear and dependency. That's why religion was invented. No one's going to obey another human being forever no matter how clever, but an invisible and all-seeing entity with the power over one's destiny? Now that's a different matter.' He regarded Emil as an atheist would a believer. 'As long as people think struggling through life as an obedient slave will eventually be rewarded, one person can control millions.'

Emil ignored the implied insult to his beliefs. 'So why are we always either at war or hell-bent on starting one?'

'Because life is not meant to be easy for anyone let alone a privileged few. A hundred thousand years of human invention cannot supplant a billion years of life struggling to survive and that instinct is so powerful, even when one of nature's creatures no longer needs to, it will *find a reason* to struggle.'

The bird won the battle and flew away with its prize. 'That thrush is no doubt off to feed its young which it would fight to the death to protect if it had to.' Mengele pointed at Emil as if it was somehow all his fault. 'And that is man's problem – making life easier should mean there's no need to fight for anything. But an instinct a billion years old says we should.' He settled back into his seat again. 'The trouble is, thanks to inventions like the hydrogen bomb, killing people has never been *easier*.'

Emil acknowledged Mengele's take on the madness of war but still wasn't interested. 'What has all that got to do with Ariloch?'

The old man hesitated before answering. 'If man's

instinct for survival could be removed then all wars would end – it's as simple as that.'

Emil frowned. 'I'm no expert, but won't removing our instinct for survival just cause us all to give up and die?'

Mengele glanced towards his kitchen. 'Would you care for a cup of coffee?'

CHAPTER FIFTEEN

Helping the world's most wanted Nazi into his house was the last thing Emil expected to have to do. Mengele clutched at his chest on the way in and Emil began to worry if the old man would even live long enough to unburden his evil.

The doctor fell rather than sat into a chair. 'My apologies – would you mind making the coffee? Black, no sugar.'

Emil cast an eye over the kitchen. Quite a contrast to what Mengele had left behind in Ariloch. The lack of Maria's touch aside, an abundance of polished copper pots above an immaculate cast-iron range were now just two tatty aluminium pans on a greasy stove. Even the water was questionable judging by the jerry can of it on the floor. Emil separated the two halves of a percolator and emptied the grounds.

'Bit of a comedown, eh? I suppose you're wondering where all the money went?' Mengele offered a cigarette and lighter. Emil took the latter.

'I'm more interested in where it came *from*.' He lit the gas.

The doctor placed the cigarette down on the table and

drew another. 'There's no money in abortion, Sergeant – illegal or otherwise. It was the spoils of war that allowed me to continue my research.' Mengele put the cigarette between his lips and waited. Emil paused before lighting it. 'But it didn't take my hosts long to realise Nazis possess something far more valuable than mere art or treasure.' His chest appeared to swell with pride as well as smoke. 'A proven ability to turn a humiliated country into a proud and powerful nation interested them far more.'

A fit of coughing interrupted the hubris but not the history lesson. 'And the world would soon need a *new* superpower.' Emil was puzzled. Mengele elaborated. 'Once Russia had demonstrated their own atomic weapon, nuclear war with North America seemed inevitable.' The doctor dug out two cups and placed them on the table. 'As South America would have been one of the few continents still standing afterwards, an opportunity to lead the world into a new beginning seemed obvious.'

'So what went wrong?' The percolator started bubbling. 'Or right I'm happy to say.'

'What still exists to this day – the *deterrent* of nuclear war.'

Emil was still perplexed. 'But that was over thirty years ago and even if the rest of the world was wiped out tomorrow, Argentina's in no position to take advantage. Why didn't Peron or the junta just get bored and hand you over to the Israelis?'

Mengele seemed to have an answer for everything.

'They did. That's how the likes of Eichmann and others were caught – by the government either turning a blind eye or actually assisting the Nazi hunters. If it wasn't for the Americans, Mossad would have got to me too.'

Emil knew he was being deliberately drawn away from his original intent but the Nazi's words were still nonetheless intriguing. And anyway, given the world's level of interest in the monster, it was probably only right someone should be able to recount his last words.

The coffee maker fell silent. Emil removed it from the stove and filled the cups. 'Americans?'

Mengele's pride made a return. 'It wasn't just Argentina's steel and mining industries that needed to join the twentieth century, the existing agriculture was just as inefficient so I used my knowledge of embryology to set about improving the country's beef exports.' Emil passed Mengele a cup. Both his hands were needed to steady it. 'And when the Americans found out cattle didn't just survive the harshest of winters but went on to produce the highest milk and beef yields they wanted to know how that was being done.' He took a sip. 'Needless to say, when they found out who was doing it, they became interested for other reasons.'

'Bullshit! I don't believe it. You're one of the world's most wanted men. If the Americans had found you, they'd have given you straight to the Israelis. It's as simple as that.'

Mengele groaned. 'We've already been through this, Sergeant. There is no such thing as good *or* evil.' He made to end the argument. 'Over a hundred thousand Jews died constructing the V2 rockets that killed a similar number of Londoners during the Blitz, and yet both countries applauded the rocket's designer when he helped put a man on the Moon.' He became cynical. 'Don't you find it strange the Israelis have never even asked let alone *demanded* the Americans repatriate Wernher Von Braun to answer for *his* war crimes?' Emil didn't respond. 'It's thanks to loyal Nazis like him, that what were once little more than big fireworks have become today's sophisticated intercontinental ballistic missiles, capable of killing millions.'

Mengele put down the cup and stubbed out what was left of his cigarette. 'So, is it really that much of a surprise to learn the Americans would want sophisticated *men* capable of killing millions too?'

CHAPTER SIXTEEN

Emil picked up the cigarette he'd been offered and lit it. He inhaled deeply while taking in the disturbing logic of Mengele's story. 'The *Americans* are protecting you.'

Mengele didn't respond.

The visitor looked at his host. 'But I didn't see anything *sophisticated* in Ariloch – cattle or otherwise. Just dead and tortured children.'

'Tortured? I appreciate you're no human rights activist, Sergeant. But tell me, just how upset and distressed were the orphans?'

It dawned on the young detective distress was the last thing the children appeared to be suffering from. If anything, they seemed unusually content with their lives – right up until the premature ending of it. The look on Emil's face answered the question. The old man got up to refill his cup.

'I know it's difficult, Sergeant, but try to see past the visually abhorrent and towards what was actually achieved – the creation of some very happy individuals.' He sat down.

Emil glared at the instigator of everything he'd been shocked by in Ariloch. 'You forgot *obedient*.'

Mengele's demeanour didn't change. 'The Americans' requirements were very specific – stronger, faster and *compliant*. What's the point of building a nation of supermen only for them to take over what they were made to defend?'

Emil was disgusted. 'I always knew the Americans were no better than the Nazis.'

'No better than other *human beings*, Sergeant. Try to remember what a hundred thousand years of evolution have turned us all into: masters and their *slaves*. Guess which group you and I belong to?' Emil became quiet again. 'If it makes you feel any better, the Americans have been just as busy experimenting on their *own* people.' Mengele lit another Marlboro while reeling off a list: 'State-sanctioned sterilisation of the insane; the testing of biological and chemical weapons on the unaware; deliberate exposure to radiation and venereal diseases – take your pick.' He became thoughtful. 'Their own pitiful attempts to produce a *pure* race of people aside, the Americans would make excellent Nazis. They're just as determined to stamp their own authority on the planet but infinitely subtler about it. Their propaganda machine is particularly effective – countries that displease them aren't invaded, they're *liberated*. Conversely, freedom fighters that rise up against a tyrannical ally are considered *terrorists* and because Uncle Sam controls most of the world's media, nobody makes a serious attempt to question anything they do.' Mengele stared into space. 'I particularly admire the way *democracy* is used as an excuse to kill thousands of people in order to *free* them. He slowly shook his head. 'Pure genius.'

Mengele's cigarettes weren't lasting long, and he put the latest one out in an ashtray. 'Which is why their disinterest in my ability to create a race of super *masters*, surprised me.'

Emil glanced at the portrait. The seven lighter faces in it became more meaningful. 'You mean Maria's brothers?'

'There's a reason why Pedro was the most non-compliant of the children – he was the last to prove the potential of not just superior strength and endurance but enhanced reasoning and thinking too.'

The policeman recalled his near-death experience. Handcuffs aside, he had always wondered how Pedro had managed to dispatch the assassins so efficiently. The question of the boy's physical appearance was about to be answered too. 'Did you deliberately stunt the orphans' growth?'

It was made to sound a necessity. 'I don't think the government – Peronist, fascist or otherwise would appreciate having twenty or so not just super strong but super intelligent men and women wandering about the countryside.'

Emil broadened the unsettling scenario. 'I should imagine that would be *every* country's nightmare.'

Mengele lit his fourth cigarette. 'Actually, no. There was one forward-thinking nation – Great Britain.'

CHAPTER SEVENTEEN

'*Britain?* What have they got to do with Argentina?' Emil considered his own question. 'Other than getting kicked out of the Malvinas once the generals have stopped sabre-rattling about it.'

'The old lion might not be what it was, but they're still a force to be reckoned with. There's a good reason why most modern armies have adopted the English model. You might be surprised at how far they would be prepared to go to maintain sovereignty over the Falkland Islands.'

'But the British Empire is dead – there's no way they'd travel 8,000 miles to defend something they don't care about anymore. The world has moved on. And theirs especially.'

Mengele presented Emil with his empty cup. He got up to make a fresh brew.

'Their empire isn't dead – it's dying. Which is why the British were more interested in my work's potential to prolong life rather than end it as violently as possible.'

'*Prolong* life? Is that what happens once you've finished killing and enslaving a third of the world?' Emil didn't bother hiding his contempt for that nation too.

'Of course. It's just another example of nature's constant need to struggle and what happens when that's no longer required.' The doctor indicated through the open door. 'What happens to plants once they've finished growing?'

The recharged percolator was placed back onto the stove. Emil looked at the various weeds and untended flora in the yard outside. 'They go to seed and die.'

'Exactly. And like every empire or old country before them, Britain has gone to seed and is now dying.' He leaned forward in his seat. 'And just like South America is mainly made up of Spain's children, North America is the offspring of Great Britain.' Emil chuckled at the ridiculous analogy.

Mengele stood his ground. 'Empires, nations, states, countries – call them what you will, they all begin and end like most of nature's creations: they're born, they grow up, pick fights with the kid next door, grow up a bit more, find someone to share their life with and then have offspring keen to find *their* way in the world.' He sat back. 'Everything eventually grows old and dies, and like the rest of Europe, Britain and Spain are living out their final days.' He took another puff of his cigarette. North and South America on the other hand, are still very much in their belligerent and ideological early twenties.'

Emil challenged the hypothesis. 'So what happened to that young upstart, *Nazi* Germany?'

The doctor shrugged. 'He bullied too many old European mothers and fathers, who asked their younger American cousins to help and they did – just as any son or daughter would do. It didn't stop the US from thinking they're the rightful heirs to the throne of the world, though if anything, winning the war reconfirmed the entitlement.'

'Do you think America would come to Britain's aid again if we were to take the Malvinas back?'

'They might do but their inheritance concerns them more and all three countries are involved in fighting the greatest threat to it – communism. I don't think they would want to jeopardise that.' Emil passed him a fresh cup of coffee. Mengele offered what he thought would be the most likely outcome. 'Like many old people determined not to show it, I think Britain would fight to retain the islands but they'd much rather persuade you to leave.'

Emil looked through the back door and towards the woods. 'Like you *persuaded* me to bury the gun?' Mengele turned his head in the same direction but didn't reply.

Emil regarded the indentations on the doctor's head and recalled the device that must have been used to create them. He shuddered and reached for his cigarettes.

'How's it done?'

The old man coughed again and got up from the chair. 'Wait here.' He went into the room next door. Emil followed him anyway.

Unsurprisingly, the main living area was just as unkempt and basic as what passed for a kitchen. No wing-backed leather suites, marble fireplaces or medical libraries doubling as studies here – just sticks of furniture amid piles of old newspapers. Mengele went through some of them. A grunt of satisfaction accompanied the rediscovery of the edition he was searching for. The shock of seeing Emil peering at him as he turned around made Mengele clutch at his chest again. 'I told you to wait in the kitchen! Here, read that.' He thrust the newspaper at him before pushing past.

Emil was disappointed. After seeing the elaborate collection of handwritten manuscripts and drawings in Ariloch, the very least he was expecting was some kind of abridged version – not a tatty old tabloid with an item ringed in ink.

'Doctors and priests hailed a miracle yesterday after mother of six, Senora Mirta Careaga, heroically rescued all of her children when their car overturned and caught fire. Incredibly, the forty-two-year-old not only managed to escape the inferno but actually lifted the vehicle off one of her children, before rescuing them all by wrenching open the doors of the twisted and burning sedan. Amazingly, only one of the family suffered any serious injury and all are expected to make a full recovery. Mama Careaga put the incredible strength needed to lift two tonnes down to healthy living and a strong belief in God.'

Emil re-entered the kitchen and placed the newspaper down on the table. 'So, you found a way to unleash superhuman strength. How does that become superhuman thought?'

The doctor tapped a finger on the news item. 'Nature's struggle for survival in action. Millions of years of evolution haven't just developed the more obvious strengths to assist that, there are hidden potentials in all of us that only reveal themselves under extreme circumstances. I made it possible for them to be used at any time.'

Mengele's pride reappeared. 'Although I'd proven the genetics required to increase the size and yield of cattle, the same studies would still be needed in humans so the Americans identified a village vulnerable enough to require not just a doctor but the resources necessary to function as a community too.'

'You mean the replacement of livestock and grain?'

Mengele nodded. 'The expectation being the villagers would willingly submit to even the most unsettling of my experiments if they also relied on me for their very existence.'

Emil's bile rose, but he had to keep it in check if he were to get to all of the truth. He offered one of his own cigarettes. Mengele's hands shook as he took it.

'But there was a problem. The Arilochians were deeply religious and even though they could be bribed to turn a blind eye to the women I artificially impregnated and then performed abortions on, the foetuses I let survive to full term were deemed to be God's *miracles* – no matter how abnormal the results.'

Mengele's speech was wavering. He must have known he would soon be dead. Emil supposed anyone in that situation would find it difficult to talk.

'The villagers had to be convinced to allow their children to be sacrificed for my work and then one day the solution presented itself.' He became silent for a moment as if having second thoughts on what to divulge. 'My early experiments had been successful enough for me to chance repeating them on an adult. The villagers may have restricted my access to children but not grown men too disabled to work the fields and when I surgically altered the backward brain of one of them, what I was anticipating happened – he became both physically *and* mentally stronger.'

'And that made the villagers trust you again?'

'No, he never left the basement. Not alive anyway.' Emil's disgust was becoming harder to control. 'Once I realised his cognitive abilities had improved I set about exploring the extent of them but when he began answering questions that hadn't even been asked...' The doctor wrung his hands as he recalled something that must have been as traumatic for him as it was for his victim. 'He couldn't just read my thoughts, he could actually explore what was in my mind and I sensed every moment of it.'

'So that's how you know so much about me. You've been reading *my* thoughts ever since I first arrived.'

The eugenicist looked towards the front of the house. 'The range is limited and it becomes harder to discern between minds when others are present. That's why I left the city – the noise created by millions of thoughts became too much for me to bear.'

Emil was keen to know the extent of the new capabilities. 'But there's a big difference between reading a mind and persuading it to do something, Mengele. How did you make me think I was in pain or to ditch the gun?'

The question seemed to be ignored. 'Once the

subject realised I didn't just abort foetuses, he fought against me, both physically *and* mentally.' The doctor looked into the back yard again. 'I was saved by what came to your rescue an hour ago – fatigue. Old age in your case but in mine, a congenital heart condition.'

'Wait a minute, are you saying these incredible abilities have limits?'

'I'm afraid so. It's all very well releasing the superman in us but there's a good reason why he's rarely seen – the body can only withstand the stress for so long.' He put a hand on his chest. 'More research is needed but I suspect it accelerates ageing too.'

Emil now knew why, along with the rest of the orphans, Pedro would soon be dead. He steadied his resolve. 'So what happened and how did that lead to *persuading* the Arilochians to give up their children again?'

'The subject suffered a cardiac arrest and died during our struggle but not before he'd made the mistake of merging with my mind completely.' Mengele appeared to deliberately stall again. 'It meant I was able to read and influence *his* thoughts too.'

The Nazi stubbed out his cigarette. Emil gave him another straight away. 'And when I realised the devout Christian interpreted my probing as some kind of divine intervention, the answer to the villagers' lack of co-operation immediately became apparent.'

Mengele put a hand to his head. 'I made him believe I was Jesus.'

CHAPTER EIGHTEEN

'He thought you were the son of God?'

'Applying the treatment to the whole village was out of the question so I decided to subject myself to it and enter the minds of the Arilochians that way. The response was instant – they thought I'd been sent from Heaven.'

Emil considered what the villagers and the Church in particular must have thought they were getting. 'The Bible's pretty specific. What happened when God's wrath *didn't* lay waste to sinners and raise the dead as a Second Coming is supposed to?'

'There's only one thing the Church wants more than biblical prophecies to come to pass and that's non-believers converted to their cause so when I convinced a few visiting communist guerrillas to lay down their arms and worship God too…'

'And the elaborate drawings detailing how to *visit* Heaven?'

Mengele seemed reluctant to answer that. 'Smoke and mirrors to assist the belief process.'

Emil put the photograph back in front of him. 'What has this got to do with Maria's brothers?'

The making of a fresh pot of coffee was encouraged. Emil knew Mengele was stalling. Wanting the last minutes of his life to last as long as possible was the only thing he couldn't be blamed for.

'Unlike the Americans, superior intelligence didn't bother the British in the slightest. In fact, replacing their entire population with intellectual as well as physically strong supermen and women appeared to be the desired outcome.'

Emil paused refilling the percolator. 'You Nazis wanted to wipe out the Jews and we're in the middle of eradicating communists, but why on earth would a country want *all* of its citizens dead?'

'I've already told you. The British Empire is dying and they wanted to put the patient out of its misery.'

Emil thought he was being made the butt of some joke. 'Nonsense! You said yourself that the British would come to the aid of the Malvinas islanders if they had to. That doesn't sound like a nation intent on wiping itself out.'

'I also said that if you did invade the Falkland Islands, they would try to persuade you to leave and that's exactly how they intend ending the humiliation and shame of losing the world's greatest ever empire – by *persuading* the current population to commit suicide so it can be replaced.'

Emil burst out laughing. 'Well, I hope they got their money back, because you quite clearly failed!'

Mengele remained stoic. 'Dropping a hydrogen bomb might produce a similar effect but it would also lay waste to everything and make the land impossible to inhabit for hundreds of years. Far better to convince everyone to take their own lives instead.'

'Well, you did a pretty good job of convincing me to try and strangle myself earlier but by your own admission, the stress causes both parties to expire well before their time so unless…' He thought again of the doctor's graphical representation of Jacob's Ladder and how it implied a subsequent return from an ascent of it. 'The dead *can* actually be raised?'

Mengele didn't answer.

Emil shook his head. 'I'm beginning to think the British, Americans and you are all as mad and as bad as each other.' Emil dismissed it all as nonsense and got back to the purpose of his mission. 'Why did you kill six of the boys?'

Mengele became nervous again. 'Because only one was needed.'

'*One* child? All that for one single superman? Why even bother?'

'God apparently thought just the one son necessary. Perhaps the British wanted their own saviour?'

Emil dismissed that blasphemy too and picked up the portrait. 'Which one?'

The boy was pointed out. 'Juan.'

At least Emil had a name to give Maria and her mother. Now to find out if he was still alive.

'Where is he?'

'Somewhere in the UK, I suppose.'

And that statement made Emil realise he now had

everything he came for. Just one job left to do. He wondered how best to ensure Mengele stayed put while the gun was retrieved. Emil was still curious about one thing, however. 'How on earth did you get the children to sit in that god-awful chair?'

Mengele may have been in fear of his life but he was still unrepentant. 'I can understand why what I've done will seem abhorrent to many but despite what's been said, I have never sought satisfaction from the suffering of others. I would have thought the orphans referring to me as 'Uncle' Joe would be enough to convince you I didn't just have the villagers' respect, I had their love too.'

Emil shifted at the uncomfortable sense of that.

'That sentiment wasn't just down to fresh grain and livestock – a steady supply of money meant the latest medical equipment and techniques. Anaesthesia and even pre-meds were always calculated to reduce anxiety to an absolute minimum.'

Emil gestured towards Mengele's scars. 'What about you? How did you manage to sedate yourself and perform surgery at the same time?'

'I didn't.'

'Then who carried out the operation?'

'My assistant.'

'Assistant? What assistant?'

The old Nazi picked up the portrait – his eyes welled.

'I think there's something Maria has yet to tell you.'

CHAPTER NINETEEN

Maria waved at Emil but he didn't respond. She ran towards him. He would have done the same and especially after not having seen her for weeks but not now.

She caught up, threw her arms around his neck and kissed him. The affection wasn't returned. She incorrectly guessed the reason why.

'Oh come on darling – cheer up. We both know why I have to go to the US but I'll be home twice a year and promise to write every week.' Maria gave Emil one of her faux 'damsel in distress' looks which usually got him smiling but not this time. Fake helplessness became a real concern.

'Darling – what's the matter?' She took his hand but it was pulled away.

'I found him.'

The concern appeared to intensify. 'Did you kill him?'

'No.'

The way Maria closed her eyes and drew a cross over her heart all but confirmed what Emil had always suspected but hoped could never be true. He coldly explained why he felt unable to keep his promise to Maria and her mother.

'I couldn't.' He swallowed the sense of betrayal. 'Because that would mean having to kill the equally guilty person that willingly assisted him.'

Maria stood back. 'What did he tell you?'

'Nothing. He said I should ask *you*.' Emil pushed his feelings for Maria to one side and became more policeman than future husband. 'Why do you think he would say that?'

There was a low wall a few feet from where they were standing and Maria dropped her head before shuffling towards it. Emil stayed where he was, determined not to react naturally to whatever she did or said next. Maria sat down but Emil stood his ground even though it pained him to do so.

She spoke. 'When you're young – and I mean really young – the world can seem a very frightening place.' She clutched at her bag as a distressed child would a soft toy. 'You wake up every morning wishing the horror that visited you the night before was actually a bad dream that won't ever happen again but it does – every night.'

Emil changed his mind and sat down next to her.

'To begin with you hope your distress and pleading will stop the pain but when it doesn't, there's only one thing a child raised to believe they are sinful can do and that's beg God for his forgiveness.' Maria looked at Emil. 'Isn't that what the Church teaches? Pray to God and you will be forgiven?'

She turned away again. 'But he didn't, which to me

meant my sin must have been so bad, only by suffering could I be redeemed from it.'

Maria reached into her purse and took out a handkerchief to dab her eyes. 'So, like the good little girl I was so desperate to become I stopped crying, stopped pleading and just stared up at the ceiling while waiting for God to decide when I'd been punished enough.'

She withdrew an old passport from her purse and opened it. 'And then one day, *he* arrived.'

Maria placed her hand on the photograph in the same way Emil had seen Mengele place his on hers.

'My first memories were of a handsome man with a seemingly bottomless pocket of candy but it was when rumours began of him being the village's saviour that his appearance from nowhere started to make sense. Not just because of the miracles he performed but how he always had time for the children.' She stared ahead. 'Just like Jesus.'

The less anxious memory appeared to calm her. 'I suppose children can easily be bought with candy but it was something far more precious that made me love him just as if he were the son of God – kindness.'

She turned to Emil again. 'Can you imagine how desperate I was for a *real* father? One that didn't hurt me or abuse my mother and brothers too?'

Emil couldn't possibly empathise with what she must have suffered but nodded anyway.

Maria chuckled through her tears. 'I must have been a real pain to Uncle Joe in those early days.' She stopped laughing. 'Any excuse to get away from *him*.'

She wiped a tear from the photograph. 'But being near Uncle Joe made me happy, so I stopped asking God for his forgiveness and began living two lives – the good of the doctor during the day and the evil that was my father by night.'

She appeared to ponder what might have been. 'And if the inevitable hadn't have happened, maybe that would still be the arrangement today.'

There was no shame in what Maria said next but she hung her head all the same. 'Just after my twelfth birthday, I fell pregnant.'

CHAPTER TWENTY

The revelation sickened Emil. He couldn't reconcile the horrors she must have suffered at the hands of her father with the horrors *her* hands must have perpetrated on others. He never thought it would be possible to both love and yet be repulsed by someone at the same time.

'My father flew into another one of his rages when he found out but to him, the solution was simple – my baby would become just another one of the many aborted foetuses Uncle Joe needed for his work.'

Maria lifted her head and looked into the distance. 'But he didn't understand the bond Uncle Joe and I had formed and what that would lead to.'

Her demeanour picked up for a moment. 'I'll never forget the way he held my hand as he not only put my mind at rest about the procedure itself but what the future held for me as his live-in housekeeper and assistant. I was so ashamed and yet at the same time so happy at the thought of actually living with the one person I knew could protect me from the evil that was my father.'

She clasped her hands together as if to plead for Emil's forgiveness. 'Can you possibly understand that?'

Emil could, but only because the alternative of perpetual incestuous rape was too horrific to contemplate. But given the notorious Nazi doctor's history, Emil could also understand why millions of others would have serious difficulty in understanding either existence.

He swallowed before speaking. 'There's a big difference between being a housekeeper and a surgeon's assistant, Maria.'

She looked down again. 'You saw the children. They plainly needed surgery after birth but the people saw those abnormalities as God-given. Uncle Joe knew how to convince both the Church and the villagers to think differently but couldn't achieve it without my help.'

All of Emil's emotions were under pressure but it was anger that boiled over first. 'They shouldn't have been born in the first place!'

Maria coldly explained the inference of Emil's disapproval. 'Like all disabled or less worthy people, you mean?'

'No, of course not. Just those conceived *unnaturally*.'

She drew a logical conclusion from that too. 'Like my father's child perhaps?' She reminded him of their faith. 'The Catholic Church views the premature termination of *any* life to be a sin no matter what was suffered in the creation of it.'

Emil became quiet. Maria concluded with the equally logical but perhaps more disturbing revelations of what Mengele required her to do.

'Uncle Joe needed to subject himself to the operation, and I assisted him.'

Emil tried not to picture what that would have entailed but then realised he'd dreamt something similar the night before the doctor's house burnt to the ground.

The scene of his beloved ramming the head-cage device down onto Mengele filled Emil's thoughts. He knew the maniacal look on Maria's face as she repeatedly drove the drill into the Nazi's skull was just part of the nightmare, but couldn't rid himself of the vision.

It had to be confronted. 'You weren't even a teenager at the time, Maria. How could you possibly do something so horrifying?'

Maria placed a hand on his forearm. She became nervous again. 'Love, Emil. Love. When a child is suddenly released from unimaginable evil you cannot help but respond with love to what enabled that.'

She moved her hand down to his. They were both trembling. 'They say one will do anything for love and it's true.'

Emil looked deep into Maria's eyes. As a homicide officer, he had always scoffed at murderers who had suggested a similar emotion lay behind their actions but he was beginning to understand how some of them could have genuinely killed for it – killed for love.

He was wondering whether his feelings for Maria could cause him to do the same when it struck him. Why else take an unregistered gun to the so-called *evil* doctor's lair?

Emil put his arm around Maria and took the passport from her.

'He cried like a baby when I showed him your picture, you know.'

Maria responded in kind and Emil pulled her closer. He bowed to both the disturbing revelations of her childhood and the love for her he had no problem understanding.

'I guess the world is not as black and white as I like to think it is.'

Maria tilted her head up and they kissed.

CHAPTER TWENTY-ONE

'You have to find him.'

'What?'

'You have to find Juan.'

'Maria, it's all but impossible to find someone missing in Argentina let alone another country.' Emil thought of the worst case. 'It's been thirteen years. He might not even be in the UK anymore – talk about looking for a needle in a haystack.'

The apparent fruitlessness didn't deter Maria. She looked up from her family's portrait. 'Then the police in England have to be contacted as soon as possible.'

Emil laughed. 'Contact the British police? Don't you read the newspapers? Their refusal to hand back the Malvinas means the junta has all but ended diplomatic relations so you can forget about any police co-operation. It has to be something pretty serious to justify contacting Interpol and I'm sorry, Maria, but the station captain would have to sanction it and I doubt Inspector Gomez would even let it get that far.'

Emil expected his fiancé to look crestfallen and an opposite reaction surprised him. 'When will you be a Captain?'

Emil became crestfallen instead. 'Maria, even if I had the necessary background, education, and political connections, it would still take at least twenty years. And that's assuming I get to the rank of Inspector first.' He put his arm around her. 'We are what we are and the situation is what it is and nothing can change that. All I know is that despite everything we've been through, we still have each other and that's the most important thing.'

Maria shrugged off the affection and stood up to face him. 'If you can't find Juan then I'm going to have to.'

Emil was about to chuckle at the ridiculous suggestion when the detective in him sensed something beyond a sisterly concern for her pseudo-sibling.

He gestured towards the portrait. 'Maria, one of the reasons why I love you so much is because, despite everything you've been through, you still care about people.'

He steeled himself for an emotionally-charged retort. 'But Juan isn't your *real* brother – he's the unnatural result of a sick experiment.'

Maria's response surprised Emil yet again. 'Tell me what Uncle Joe talked about.'

Something told Emil his love was seeking more than just a family reunion.

A disturbing thought came to him. 'Did *you* perform the brain operations on Juan and the boys?'

'No, I thought their health would ensure an escape from all that but the moment I saw their bones I knew then what I feared most had actually happened.'

She repeated the question. 'What did the doctor and you discuss *exactly*?'

Emil sighed. 'I went there to kill him, Maria. Not to have a chat.'

She sat down next to him. 'But you didn't and despite what you say, your change of heart has nothing to do with me being his assistant. What did he tell you about his work?'

'Nothing that's not either well documented or you and I haven't seen with our own eyes.' Emil slowly shook his head. 'Pure horror.'

'I'm not talking about Auschwitz or Ariloch. You didn't kill him because he made you question your own ethics.'

Given the seedier side to Emil's job as a policeman, Maria was encroaching on territory he would rather she didn't and it made him feel uncomfortable. 'I'll admit I'm no angel, Maria but if you insist on comparing my failings with those of an evil Nazi, then we need to have a serious talk.'

'He didn't just talk about *your* limitations, Emil – he made you see the failings in all of us.'

Emil was about to scoff when he picked up on the connection being made. 'According to Mengele, both the Americans and the British employed him to assist their own eugenics programmes but for different reasons.'

Maria concurred. 'Like the Nazis, the Americans want to build a master race but the British want the exact opposite – a nation of *slaves*.'

Emil regarded her as if she were as mad as the doctor.

'Why would anyone use something capable of making them invincible create a nation of unthinking sheep instead?'

'Because sheep are easier to control especially when it comes to slaughtering them. They'll happily get in line at the abattoir.'

Maria made the method of population control sound like a more efficient but just as disturbing version of Hitler's 'Final Solution'.

Emil couldn't take it in. 'Mengele likened the British Empire to a plant that had gone to seed and was now dying.' He turned to her again. 'Are you saying Juan was made to end his own life? It doesn't make any sense.'

'He wasn't bred to be a sheep.' Maria turned to face Emil and tried to make what she had to say sound plausible. 'He's the shepherd.'

1985

CHAPTER TWENTY-TWO

'Inspector Vazquez?'

Emil looked at his Sergeant.

'There's a lady in reception who says she knows you – a Doctor Maria Fierro.'

Emil's stomach tightened. Six years since he had last heard that name. Six years since he last saw her. Six years since they promised each other they would marry just as soon as she had returned from North America.

'Show her in.'

The tightness became nausea. Emil distracted himself by tidying the desk but the rattle of a cup against its saucer made his nervousness plain. He put both down and grabbed his fingers to try to stop them from shaking when the only woman he had ever wanted to spend the rest of his life with, appeared. He stood up.

It was like meeting for the first time. He blushed. So did she.

'Shall I close the door, boss?'

Emil didn't respond. The sergeant looked at them both staring at each other. He raised his eyebrows before closing it anyway.

The noise of the door shutting broke their trance-like state. They began talking over each other. When it became clear Maria was just as anxious, Emil raised his hands to end the incoherence. 'First things first.' He walked around his desk and pulled up a chair. 'Please, have a seat.' The smell of her perfume as she sat down made him close his eyes. He opened them again, took a deep breath and walked back to his side of the desk.

'Can I get you a coffee or something?' Emil hoped the tone of the question was appropriate given their history. Whatever 'appropriate' meant.

'You haven't changed one bit.' The passing years hadn't diminished the power of Maria's smile either and Emil fought against folding in the presence of it.

He took another deep breath before tapping his expanding girth with both hands. 'Well, if this isn't obvious then the receding hairline and moustache must be.' His fingers ran through and down both thickets. 'You, on the other hand, are exactly the same.' Emil wasn't joking. Maria could still pass for the twenty-five-year-old she was when they first met.

The visitor surveyed her surroundings. 'So, you made it then.'

Emil did the same. 'Nothing's changed. Inspector is probably my ceiling. Although I see you achieved Padre Martin's hopes for you – Doctor.'

'Pathology at the moment, but I hope to specialise in paediatrics eventually.'

Emil asked the question he had to. 'Married?' She shook her head before asking him the same. He shook his head too. 'How's your mother?'

'She's fine.'

And that just about brought them both up to date. Emil's nervousness ended but only to be replaced by bitterness. He had difficulty in not letting his words sound resentful. 'Why Maria? Why did you stop replying to my letters?'

The love of his life dropped her chin. 'Please don't, Emil. It's too painful.'

'Too painful? Then why are you here? To torment me? You know how I felt about you.' He hesitated before adding, 'How I've always felt about you.'

Maria pulled herself together and sat up. 'I'm here on official business. I'm part of the team that's investigating the junta's war crimes and we don't want the police arresting us when we start digging up graves in search of *the disappeared*.'

Her words seemed out of context but Emil knew she was serious. He'd been expecting something similar ever since the junta had been ousted and a new government elected on a promise of *truth and reconciliation*. He'd only been a pawn in the fascists' determination to rid the country of the left and certainly hadn't killed anybody, but the ranks of those imprisoned was steadily being reduced, hence Gomez having to replace the station captain and Emil's early promotion to inspector. He often recalled what Mengele had to say about the subjectivity of good and evil and wondered if he ought to prepare himself for an imminent escape to Brazil or Chile just in case.

Despite the mixed feelings, Emil forced himself to

do his job. 'The police will give you whatever assistance you need, Doctor. We certainly won't arrest anyone for desecrating a grave. Just make sure your colleagues have the necessary documentation.' They half-smiled at each other.

Maria became visibly more uncomfortable. 'There's something else.' She appeared reluctant to look Emil in the eye. 'Ariloch doesn't come under our jurisdiction but I require the same access.'

Emil didn't need to be a police inspector to recognise an ulterior motive when he saw one. 'What for?'

'I need to take samples from some of the graves there too.'

'But you've just told me Ariloch doesn't form part of the commission's remit so why?'

'Have you heard of 'DNA'?' Emil hadn't. Maria explained. 'It's a bit like the body's fingerprint. Only you don't need a living finger to prove someone's identity – just a small tissue sample like a fragment of bone.

Emil rolled his eyes, stood up and reached for his cigarettes. 'For God's sake, Maria, are you still trying to find your brother?'

Maria talked as if the last six years had never happened. 'He has to be found, Emil, and DNA could help with that.' The inspector offered a cigarette to the only woman he had ever loved. She refused it. 'There's talk of producing a database of everyone's DNA. Unlike fingerprints, family members can be identified using it. If I can get a sample from one of my brothers I can add it to the database and if ever Juan's is added too, we'll be able to find him.'

Emil inhaled from the Marlboro. 'There are a lot of 'ifs' in there, Maria. Getting the piece of bone you require won't be a problem and I guess adding whatever you get from it to some kind of database won't be an issue either. But even if the same is done at the other end, all that will prove is that Juan is dead.'

'Only a sample of saliva is needed from a living person and police in the UK have started taking swabs whenever they make an arrest.'

Emil scoffed. 'So, we're back to contacting the British again.' He sat down. 'In case you didn't notice, they kicked our asses out of the Malvinas a couple of years back so if relations with the UK were complicated before they're all but impossible now. And anyway, I would have thought the nature of their victory all but proves they're still an evil empire hell-bent on conquering land that doesn't belong to them – hardly a nation of sheep waiting to be led to the slaughter.'

Maria gave him a look of disapproval. 'Hmmm. I should imagine my Pampas forebears thought exactly the same when the Spanish conquistadors first invaded what eventually became Argentina but we mustn't let political differences get in the way of our relationship.'

Emil ignored the historical irony and jumped on her last word. 'And what exactly is our *relationship*?'

Maria put her head down again. 'You can do much better than me, Emil.'

'What are you talking about? You can't still be worried about our race differences – it's the 1980s, not the 1880s and you're more professionally qualified than

I'll ever be. A few racist bigots might still exist but things are changing rapidly—'

She interrupted him. 'You need someone who can give you children, Emil, and I will never be able to do that.'

PART TWO

2026

CHAPTER ONE

'Stop looking at porn.'

'I'm not.'

'I bet you were before I came in.' Tracy put the shopping on the dining table and sat down next to her fiancé. James ignored her and continued to read the web page. She tutted with exasperation. 'You're obsessed with Professor Savage – what is it this time?'

The doctor scrolled to the top. 'His peer review of *Genetic disorders in remote communities*.'

The nurse shook her head, got back up and started unpacking. 'And does he mention his evil plan to take over the world?' James sat back and narrowed his lips.

'You wouldn't be quite so flippant if you'd been there and seen the look on his face when he talked about, not being "interested" in dementia.'

Tracy picked up a bag of groceries and took them into the kitchen area. 'So you keep telling me – along with the one about rational suicide not being a choice at all.'

It had been four months since James ended his confrontation with Savage by storming out, and just a week since the last of the original fifteen Alzheimer's patients had died – of old age. In the end, only two of the trial subjects had been fit enough to travel to Switzerland for 'voluntary' euthanasia, but the doctor's final report made it clear he considered the treatment to blame.

But that was academic now. The newspapers had long since stopped vilifying the professor about *the unfortunate side-effect*. And although the BBC and other news agencies would occasionally interview senior members of the clergy and other concerned individuals, it was evident society as a whole supported his work. Tracy's attitude to the situation was typical.

'Anyway, surely a few more years of quality outweighs ten or twenty as a vegetable? I'd go for the treatment like a shot if I were diagnosed with Alzheimer's.' She came out of the kitchen. 'What does it matter if you want to kill yourself at some point afterwards? We've all got to go sometime and I'd rather not as a dribbling mess thank you very much.'

James grimaced as their main topic of conversation began again. 'You saw the evidence for yourself – you were the one who actually worked it out for goodness sake. He's found a way to surgically alter the way people think. Why doesn't that ring any alarm bells with you?'

Tracy folded her arms. 'Because he clearly has a conscience about it. Why else would he tell the world?'

Something on the television caught her eye. It was switched on with the sound muted. The twenty-four-hour news channel didn't feature the professor himself but subtitles made it clear one of the benefits he'd promised was starting to bear fruit – the words, *Multi-billion-dollar sale of dementia drug to the USA* scrolled along the bottom.

'Now that's just awful. What *is* the government supposed to do with billions of pounds it wasn't expecting? It will ruin their spending plans.'

James scoffed. 'The world may know about the treatment for Alzheimer's, but not the brainwashing. And my report into the outcome of *that* trial won't go unnoticed, I can tell you.'

Tracy became serious. 'So you've decided to accept his offer?'

James may have had severe misgivings with the professor's ethics, but it was clear those concerns weren't reciprocated. In fact, Savage had gone out of his way to show how much he still valued the psychologist's contribution – even to the point of making a joke about needing "someone to keep an eye on me". The outcome was an offer to conduct and report on the next clinical trial – *Post-operative cognitive behavioural changes observed in convicted criminals.*

He sheepishly peered at Tracy over the top of the computer screen. 'We begin selecting the lucky volunteers in the New Year.'

The words produced an explosion of excitement. 'YES!' Tracy leapt on him, planting as many kisses as possible. 'Oh, darling, you've no idea how worried I've been. I really thought you were going to resign or get fired or something.'

James pretended not to enjoy the attention. 'Well, if I really was a man of principle I'd have resigned there and then.' He gave in to Tracy and they kissed. 'But I suppose I have more important things to consider.'

Tracy pursed her lips. 'Don't let a little thing like starting a family get in the way of your anally-retentive standards. If you think saying no to the most powerful man in medicine won't affect your chances of getting a job elsewhere, then go right ahead and tell him to stick the trial right up his arse.'

'*Arse?* Not a medical term I'm familiar with, I'm afraid. And I'm not sure if I want my children repeating it, either.' He tickled her. She playfully punched him to escape and went back to the shopping.

James studied the web page again. 'So how come the most powerful man in medicine has the weakest presence on the web?'

Tracy selected one of the bags and took it to the bedroom. She stopped to view the screen on the way. 'What now?'

'Well, other than all the media stuff from the Alzheimer's trial, there's next to nothing about him – professional or otherwise. Little more than a list of educational achievements, his knighthood, other awards and where he's currently practising.' He maximised another web page. 'The search results of his peers are far more comprehensive: research conducted, results published, boards chaired – that sort of thing.'

'What's your point?'

'My point is, all the other professors seem to have followed a conventional career path, but it would appear Sir John has done anything but.'

Tracy raised her eyebrows and went into the bedroom. She half-closed the door. 'Maybe he doesn't want to show off about it, unlike the rest of them.'

'Hmmm, but he's hardly the wallflower type so I logged on the internal websites of the hospitals, universities and research centres he's worked at for evidence of his meteoric rise to stardom.'

Tracy poked her head around the door. 'And?'

'Nothing. No research, no articles, no papers – nothing he's personally published at all. There's plenty from the researchers and scientists at the pharmaceutical companies he owns, such as computer modelling of the drug but it's the surgical procedure itself which is conspicuous by its absence.' He peered into the distance. 'Where and how did he learn that? Where's the animal testing and initial human studies that must have been carried out *before* the Alzheimer's trial? No one gets the kind of results we did without a series of hit and misses first so where's the documentary evidence for that?'

He turned to face Tracy. 'A discovery that could fundamentally alter the course of human evolution seems to have magically appeared overnight.'

Tracy tutted and disappeared into the room again. 'Perhaps it did.'

James' shoulders sagged at her inability to see the unusual, not to mention concerning, in what he was trying to say. He got up from the chair and went to join her. The door was closed in his face.

'You can't come in, I'm getting changed.'

'Since when did you become so shy?'

'I'm not. I've bought a new dress and I want it to be a surprise for you.'

James was too preoccupied to think about haute couture. He turned around to look at the television but his mind was elsewhere.

'Sir John's work must have been reviewed and accepted by his peers otherwise the Alzheimer's trial would never have been allowed to go ahead. It must be classified at a level beyond the typical medical or industrial.'

He looked at the computer screen again. 'I can understand why the science of how to change the Dalai Lama into Hitler would need to be kept a secret, but the professor's personal history? Why remove that too?' He heard the bedroom door open.

'Excuse me, Headmaster.'

James turned to Tracy and gawped.

She lowered her chin and looked coyly up at him through the fringe of her pigtails. 'I'm terribly sorry to bother you, Sir, but I seem to have forgotten what the regulation length of my skirt should be.' She licked her lips as the hem of the school uniform was raised, revealing something else she'd 'forgotten'. 'Is this too short?'

James swallowed what was pooling in his mouth and responded to her allure – the feeling of being bent to

Tracy's will increased with every step. He stood in front of her like a salivating puppy. The Siren then took her pet's paws and placed them on bare flesh.

James pitifully acknowledged how well Tracy knew him. 'Why must you keep torturing me like this?'

2027

CHAPTER TWO

'Okay. I enjoyed smashing their skulls in. So what? You're going to fix that, right?'

Doctor Adams raised a hand to stop the prisoner from saying anything further. 'I have to warn you again that if you insist on revealing your crime, you will no longer be considered suitable for the trial.'

James glanced in frustration at Alex before asking the warder if the inmate could be taken outside. He turned to the MP as soon as they'd left the room.

'Ms Salib, with all due respect, I *must* insist you allow me to assess the fitness of the volunteer without further interruption. Your knowledge of the subject's crime was required at his initial selection, but the final decision is mine and, for objectivity reasons, it's important I have no understanding of what this man has done in case it prejudices my opinion. I'm simply here to ensure he has the capacity to agree taking part in the trial. Have I made myself clear?'

Alex glanced at the Conservative backbencher chosen to witness the final stage of the selection process with her. He looked blankly back.

Alex knew she'd overstepped her remit by demanding

the prisoner explain why he had taken a hammer to each of his victims, but coming face to face with some of the country's vilest offenders was tougher than she thought it would be.

The selection process itself had been a walk in the park by comparison. Of the thousands of convicted criminals put forward by the Home Office, the cross-party committee she chaired had reduced them to less than a hundred and these face to face interviews would further refine that figure to the fifteen required.

She recalled her part in getting this far. The government had been determined to use Savage's discovery as a tool in the fight against terrorism, but Alex knew the inclusion of so-called 'hate' preachers and volunteer fighters returning from the Middle East was out of the question as no matter how well intentioned, it unfairly singled out the Islamic community. She prided herself on convincing the committee the Home Office's requirement amounted to little more than racial profiling which was illegal anyway.

Alex was disappointed but not surprised to find similar attitudes prevailed towards the female prisoners the government had recommended. The endemic sexism towards them was quite staggering. Women didn't commit murder as violently as men and they certainly didn't rape in the same brutal way.

To her, it was logical. The final selection should be made up exclusively of male prisoners. The fact there were no black, Asian, Muslim, gay, transgender or any other representations from vulnerable groups was academic – white men simply made up the majority of the prison population.

But she now had to witness the interviews and the disgust that created within her was difficult to control. Alex wondered if it wasn't too late to replace Adams with a female psychologist, preferably from one of the rarer minorities and with some kind of impairment which was visible but didn't interfere too much with her duties. Alex would look into that later but decided to relent for now. She gestured for the prisoner to be readmitted.

James noticed the handcuffs and chain to the guard remained in place after the volunteer was reseated. Whatever this man had been found guilty of, he was clearly violent, which made him ideal for the purposes of the trial – the absence of any anger or loss of control after surgery would make success easier to judge. James made a note in the prisoner's file before addressing him again.

'We were discussing the surgery you would be required to undertake as part of the trial. You must understand and be prepared to accept the consequences of it. The operation involves making physical changes to your brain that will cause you to act and think differently. This is known as cognitive behaviour and yours will become markedly affected. The process is irreversible and effectively results in the creation of a new person. Although this new individual is highly unlikely to offend again, the memories and recollections of the old you will be retained which could cause a great deal of distress as you come to terms with it. Do you understand that?'

The prisoner sneered at the representatives of an establishment he clearly despised. 'Look, Doc, I've got at least another twenty years in this shithole. If a bit of my brain has to be fried to get me out of it, then that's fine by me.'

The complete absence of remorse would be the kiss of death to his freedom were the convict in front of a parole board, but once again that callousness made him the perfect candidate here. The doctor marked another positive entry, and was about to move on to the next question when the offender turned to Alex and blew her a kiss. Her reaction was seismic.

'You fucking scum! They were only babies! You raped and smashed the skulls of babies!'

The two prison warders moved closer to their charge while he grinned which incensed Alex even more.

'You vile, sick paedo! You enjoyed every second of it – didn't you? You should have been put down at birth.' She gripped the arms of her wheelchair. *'All men should be put down at birth!'*

That last comment wiped the smile off her tormentor's face. He became quizzical, as did all the others in the room.

Her outburst had changed the atmosphere and Alex stared back at each of them. She then put her head down and shed what were obviously crocodile tears. 'Those poor, poor children. Why? Why?'

The doctor motioned for the warders to take the

prisoner away. He closed the volunteer's file, picked up a black marker, removed the lid and stroked the pen from bottom left to top right across the front of it. The Tory MP got up and offered a handkerchief to his opposite backbencher.

James tried to feel just as sorry for Alex, but somehow couldn't.

CHAPTER THREE

Professor Savage shovelled the soil on top and patted it down. He checked the progress of the other seeds he'd planted and smiled as the first of the tiny green shoots he was expecting began to surface. He stood back from the pots and tried to visualise how they would look once fully grown – the plants and flowers would complement his tropical fish nicely.

The intercom interrupted. 'Doctor Adams to see you, Sir John.'

The professor acknowledged his personal assistant before picking up that morning's post. The letter on top was from the Nobel Prize Committee. There was a knock on the door and it opened.

'Ah, James. Do come in. I'm looking forward to hearing news on the selection process.' Savage offered a seat and sat down at his desk opposite.

The doctor placed the list of volunteers in front of his superior. 'Well, we have the fifteen test subjects, Sir John. But I have to say from a scientific point of view they're far from ideal. No convicted terrorists or hardened criminals – just sex offenders, and white male ones at that.'

'I thought you didn't wish to know their convictions in case it prejudiced your opinions?' The psychologist explained why that particular professional requirement had to be sidelined.

'Thanks to Ms Salib's inability to conceal her strident views, I'm afraid it became impossible to apply. Nearly every applicant deemed acceptable by her Conservative opposite had an ethnical or minority interest that made them too politically sensitive in her view which inevitably meant having to select exclusively from white males. Even then, she took it upon herself to approve only those most repellent to her – hence they're all sex offenders.'

'Well, without wishing to say, "I told you" I did anticipate as such.'

James broke away from the purpose of the meeting. 'Sir John, you know how concerned I am with the treatment but why involve someone so obviously incapable of viewing it objectively? She clearly holds men in contempt and seems to find it difficult not to express those feelings. Some of her comments during the interviews were unwelcome to say the least.'

Savage got up and walked over to the window. His office had an uninterrupted view of virgin scrub, moors and woodland that could be seen all the way to the horizon. It helped him to imagine the world the likes of Alex Salib craved.

'You two are more alike than you know.' He wandered back to his desk. 'All great discoveries should be surrounded by a healthy dose of cynicism. It forces the discoverer to constantly question his or her work, which keeps them rooted in reality. Ms Salib is just as concerned with where the treatment is heading but at the same time can't resist using it for her own purposes. The trick is to balance the development of a discovery that clearly has the power to do evil, with the needs of a society with some tough questions to answer.' He paused to allow the doctor to comment.

'Which is presumably why you deliberately made the Alzheimer patients choose suicide once they'd recovered because society can no longer afford to pay for their care.'

'Conject as much as you wish, James, but it's now a tool our elected leaders use to manage our final years in the least offensive way, nothing more and as unpalatable as it sounds, society is accepting it and so should you. Which brings me to a greater concern the people have.' He indicated the list of volunteers.

'Ms Salib may find it difficult to conceal her feminist credentials, but for the purpose of the upcoming trial she's very much in tune with the rest of the country. Paedophilia is not only on the rise but like Alzheimer's before has no cure. Unlike the dementia patients however, turning fifteen of the most dangerous and despised individuals into law-abiding citizens with healthy sexual appetites won't be in the least bit controversial – the fact there are no black, female or impaired participants amongst them to muddy the political waters just makes that certainty all the more likely.' He sat back in his chair. 'One step at a time, Doctor. Succeed in this and *all* crime will soon be a thing of the past, regardless of Alex's misguided attempts to protect the minorities who may or may not be involved in any wrongdoing.'

James raised the other issue that was bothering him. 'Sir John, where did you first practise the surgery? I've searched on line for details of the research that must have taken place prior to the Alzheimer's trial but it's conspicuous by its absence. There's plenty on the development of the drug but little else. According to the internet you didn't even go from theory to prac—'

The intercom interrupted. 'Yes? What is it, Caroline?'

There was an element of concern in her voice. 'Some police officers are on their way up, Sir John.'

The professor groaned. 'Doesn't Ms Salib ever give up?' James asked if he should leave, but the neurosurgeon told him to remain seated. A short while later, the PA ushered the men into the office and then left.

The senior of the four spoke. 'Which one of you is James Edward Adams?' The doctor stood up. 'Is there somewhere private we could talk?' James glanced at the professor before answering.

'I have nothing to hide. You can say what you have to here.' The policeman took out a notebook and read from it.

'On the eighteenth of September last year, a file being monitored by German police was accessed by a computer, the IP of which was registered in the name of a James Edward Adams. The file contained an image of a child being sexually abused.' He closed the notebook.

'James Edward Adams. I'm arresting you on the

suspicion of making and possessing an indecent image and it is my duty to inform you that you do not have to say anything but anything you do say could be used in evidence against you.'

CHAPTER FOUR

James entered the flat. Tracy was still at work – thank goodness. He gave the apartment the once-over to confirm that the police had been true to their word. They had. Other than the absence of his laptop, the flat was exactly as he'd left it that morning. Probably cleaner.

Six hours. That's how long they had kept him waiting in a police cell before the 'no comment' interview the duty solicitor had advised him to give.

Six hours. Long enough to think about the consequences. But how? How could his computer have downloaded a file without his knowledge? His private interests had caused him to view the more unsavoury side of life but nothing illegal. How could it possibly be there? His sexual fantasies certainly bordered on the uncomfortable, but as a psychologist, he'd analysed himself enough to know the boundaries of his predilections stopped well short of anything abnormal. But role play featured heavily and 'back to school' was at the top of those desires. Throw in Tracy's amateur diagnosis of his 'obsession' with internet pornography, and maybe there was a crash waiting to happen.

A crash; an understatement if ever there was one. James was no expert in criminal law but he had seen or heard enough to know what even an accusation could mean and especially for someone like him; end of reputation, career, pension – everything he'd ever worked or hoped for. Even his relationship with Tracy wasn't safe anymore. Would she even stand by him let alone still want to get married? She loved him, but would that survive once he'd been found guilty of one of society's most heinous crimes?

It didn't matter he had no sexual interest in minors, the world would soon find out that in exploring the boundaries of his legal fantasies, he'd somehow come into the possession of the worst imagery possible and would be judged by that alone. He would forever more be known as a paedophile.

James sat down. He didn't bother trying to stop the tears. Maybe it would be best to end it all and right now. He looked at the balcony.

The doorbell rang. James wanted his existence to cease there and then, but decades of middle-class conformity ensured it was answered as promptly as ever. There was no hiding his distress.

'Now, come along old chap. Where's your fighting spirit? You've never struck me as the kind to shy away from a challenge.'

Savage strolled uninvited into the centre of the apartment. He gave it a cursory glance before checking the view. The Houses of Parliament could be seen behind the block of flats in front.

'Don't the chimes of Big Ben keep you awake at night?' The professor ignored the accepted conventions of a social visit and opened the doors to a cabinet. 'Not that a good night's sleep is top of your agenda right now.' He paused before adding, 'Certainly not one you intend waking up from.' The cupboard contained volumes of text on cognitive psychology. 'I don't suppose you have any whisky?'

Playing the genial host was the last thing on James' mind and he gestured towards the kitchen on his way to the balcony. He slid open the glass door, stepped out onto it and leaned over the parapet. Would eight floors be enough?

Savage joined him. He tasted the contents of the glass he was holding and winced. 'Don't suppose you have a single malt, perchance?' The doctor didn't answer.

Savage leaned over the balcony too but then looked up. 'Methinks another two floors will be needed if you're to avoid ending up in something Ms Salib uses for transport.'

The possibility of that made the doctor stand back.

'Mind you, if you stood rather than sat, the extra couple of feet might just be enough.' Before he could be stopped, the professor did something as unexpected as it was extraordinary – he jumped up and stood on the parapet. 'Oh, yes. Maybe a little leap up too, just to be sure.'

James made to grab the madman as he appeared to be about to do exactly that. To his shock, he found himself being hauled up to join him. James was just about to force the two of them back to safety when the jacket he was wearing tightened around his chest and the next thing James knew, he was being held out in mid-air by the lapels of it – with just one hand.

'What do you say, James? I help you make up your mind or…' The professor looked at the pedestrians eight levels beneath '… I help you make up your mind?'

It was either shock, the constriction of the jacket around his neck or a combination of the two, but James was speechless. Expecting to be dropped at any moment, he grabbed the professor's arm with both hands – it was rock-solid. Like hanging from a steel girder.

Savage took another sip of his whisky. He grimaced before emptying the blend of inferior malts out onto the street below. James was returned to the balcony.

The doctor collapsed and dug his fingers into the neck of his shirt so he could breathe again. The professor sauntered back to the kitchen as if holding fourteen-stones of fully-grown man at arm's-length was something he did every day.

James looked at the parapet they, or rather one of them, had been standing on in stunned disbelief – a man in his mid sixties hadn't just demonstrated strength beyond the bounds of most Olympian weightlifters, but had done so on a four-inch wide ledge with James Adams in one hand, and Johnnie Walker in the other! James' heart rate refused to settle until what he'd just experienced sank in and that was taking its time. A nudge to his shoulder made him turn towards the glass of water being offered. He took it.

The professor pulled up a chair and sat down. 'So, how bad is it? I managed to convince the hospital staff the impounding of your work computer by the police was another example of Ms Salib's personal vendetta against me, but it's only a matter of time before the truth comes out so you'd better tell me what they're going to find.'

His still-shocked colleague gave the only piece of good news he had. 'Nothing. I confine my, er, habit to when I'm at home so there's nothing there shouldn't be in the hospital.'

'And just how addictive is this, "habit"?'

James told him everything. It seemed strange to be the one pouring his heart out and especially to someone he had so many issues with, but there was also a relief to unburdening his thoughts – just as his own patients did with him. James became more rational but just as fatalistic.

'What's going to happen to me?'

'Well, my barrister friend tells me if the police find what I fear they will then you're looking at anything up to five years.' The potential convict put his head in his hands. 'You'll be struck off before then of course and any meaningful employment afterwards will be hampered by a lifetime on the sex offenders' register.' The professor bent to his level. 'But that's just the ramifications for you, personally. Have you thought about the difficult decision Ms Roberts will have to take?'

James looked at him as if he were encroaching on to something he'd no right to. 'What do you mean?'

'You used to babysit her when she was a child so I assume her wanting to marry you now means nothing untoward happened then, but that's not the point – your conviction will be poison to her career if she continues to associate with you.' Savage sat back again. 'The same goes for your friends and colleagues especially those with children or occupations that involve them. They'll have to abandon you. Even I will be forced to publicly denounce what you've done in order to maintain the integrity of *my* reputation. Not to mention the validity of the hospital's work.' He glanced around as if to ensure no one was listening. 'I'm afraid the less savoury elements of society are quick to shout "paedophile ring" and the tabloids will be just as judgmental.'

James lay down on the floor of the balcony and sobbed. The professor let the full impact of his prognosis sink in. He then got up, placed both hands on the parapet and looked up at the night sky.

'Of course, it doesn't have to be this way.'

The doctor was in a bad place. A very bad place – the worst he'd experienced in his forty-five years, but seized the glimmer of hope that appeared to be on offer.

'What do you mean?' He dried his eyes as he got up. 'Tell me what I have to do!'

Ignoring the firm grip on his arm, Savage continued to study the heavens while explaining it.

'The courts will want to see you've come to terms with your offence and have undergone some kind of therapy to ensure it's not repeated. But they, you and I all know that paedophilia cannot be talked out of, so the chances of it reducing the length of your incarceration will be limited.'

James squeezed the professor's arm tighter. 'But I'm NOT a paedophile!' Savage waited to be released.

'I know it's difficult, but try to see it from the view of others. You could be the most asexual man on the planet, but anything other than total contrition will be seen as an arrogant disregard for people's feelings, not to mention the suffering of the child in the image. Protesting your innocence of the vile practice itself is academic – no matter how true.'

'Then it's hopeless.' The condemned man slumped onto the parapet.

'Not if you agree to take part in the trial.'

James jerked his head up. He ran his fingers through his hair just in case the operation had already been performed without him knowing. The look he gave his superior had nothing to do with contrition – or despair for that matter.

'Absolutely not! Not a hope in hell's chance – if you think I would actually *volunteer* to have my behaviour changed surgically just so you can brainwash me into doing something 'rational' then you've got another thing coming.' He scoffed with disgust. 'I don't know what goes on in your mind, Professor, but the thought of allowing you access to mine fills me with horror – what's to stop you from making me want to commit so-called 'voluntary' euthanasia like the Alzheimer's patients?'

Savage stopped stargazing, and looked down onto the street. 'I'm sorry, I didn't realise you were contemplating walking on air just now. Had I known that, I would have let go.'

James became silent as a disturbing link between his intentions and the identical plans of the dementia patients emerged. The professor turned to him.

'What have I got to do to prove to you the treatment doesn't *make* anyone do anything, James? It merely enables a greater awareness of the world and the subject's place within it. If an individual then chooses to end their existence, it's because they now have a better understanding of life and its meaning. There's nothing sinister about it.'

He reiterated the choice he was offering. 'It's up to you, James – live the rest of your life in the shadows or prove to everyone how much you've really changed. I can't guarantee it will keep you out of prison, or convince Tracy to stand by you but it might just give you a reason to carry on living.'

Adams examined his Hobson's choice. 'But what about my reputation? You might be able to keep me out of prison, save my career and marriage, but a conviction will be public knowledge. And even I wouldn't deliberately choose to see a psychologist with a criminal record, let alone one with such offensive connotations. No medical establishment in its right mind would employ me.'

Savage smiled. 'Then we'll just have to ensure everyone is in the *wrong* mind, won't we?'

James thought that a strange thing to say but bowed to his only serious option – certainly one that didn't result in a body on the pavement below. Despite his serious misgivings with the treatment, he was almost pleased to be given the alternative – the professor's powers of persuasion easily matched his physical strength. James ran his hand along the narrow edge of the parapet and wondered how someone could even stand there let alone do what Savage did.

'How did you do that?' James considered the physics required to hold a man off the ground at arm's length – it took more than strength alone. 'You leapt straight up at least four feet and the top is not just narrow but curved too. Why on earth didn't we fall to our deaths?'

The professor studied the parapet. 'A useful parlour trick for when there's a point to be made.' He grinned at his latest volunteer. 'I'll teach it to you.'

CHAPTER FIVE

'I told you. I told you internet porn would get you into trouble. Why didn't you listen to me?'

James hung his head in shame. He'd informed Tracy of his arrest the moment she walked through the door, but it was clear by her less-than-devastated reaction to it that she was either in shock or didn't appreciate the life-changing consequences – for both of them.

'Darling, I could go to prison.'

His fiancée regarded him as if he was making some kind of sick joke. 'That's nonsense. There has to be a connection with children and you're nothing like that. The police will soon realise you're just some stupid idiot who doesn't know when to stop searching for schoolgirl porn. You'll get a warning or something.'

Tracy sat down. There was an element of denial in what she'd said, and James needed her to understand the full impact of his actions – no matter how painful.

'There's no difference as far as the law is concerned, Tracy. The courts see it as encouraging abuse. I'm in serious trouble.'

She stood up. 'Then how the hell did it come to be

there in the first place? Look at me and tell me you didn't *deliberately* download it!'

James took his turn on the couch. 'I've never searched let alone downloaded anything like that, Tracy, which is why I can't understand it. Somehow my use of the internet has caused something with just about the most serious consequences possible.' He looked at her. 'For both of us.'

'What do you mean *both* of us? I had nothing to do with it!'

James already hated himself, but those feelings would reach new depths once he'd finished explaining the potential damage – especially if the newspapers got a hold of the story. She burst into tears the moment he had finished explaining it.

'You've ruined *everything*!' Tracy ran into the bedroom and threw herself onto the bed.

Without the professor's offer, James might have headed straight for the balcony again but it was the one thing stopping the situation from being utterly hopeless. He entered the bedroom and put a hand on her shoulder. Tracy shrugged it off and persisted with bawling into the pillow.

'Darling, I've been offered something that could be a way out of all this.' Tracy didn't respond. 'If I were able to prove to the courts that my mind had been *cured* of what led me to break the law, then the consequences of what I've done could be limited – I may not have to go to prison after all.'

Tracy broke away from her distress. 'How?' James

explained Savage's solution. It made her sit up. Emotional pain became a fearful concern. 'But what if you decide to commit suicide afterwards like the Alzheimer's patients?'

'I think I may have been wrong to conclude Sir John had deliberately engineered voluntary euthanasia as some sinister form of population control.' He got up from the bed. 'The treatment seems to instil some kind of enhanced ability to reason. I can't explain it – understandably, my mind has been elsewhere, but I don't think the dementia patients were *made* to want to commit suicide – they actually appear to have genuinely worked it out as the most logical thing for them to do.'

The explanation didn't reassure Tracy. 'But I want James Adams back afterwards, not Mr Spock.'

He forced a smile. 'I don't think the dramatic, political, and religious changes we saw in the dementia patients will happen again either. It was just the professor's unsettling way of refining the technique. He genuinely appears to want to rid the world of crime – hence the next trial of convicts hoping to turn over a new leaf. Although the irony of them all being sex offenders isn't lost on me.'

Tracy got off the bed. 'Darling, I'm worried. Supposing it results in some kind of chemical castration?'

'No. It's nothing like that.'

At least that was what he hoped.

CHAPTER SIX

'May I ask how tall you are, Sir John?'

Savage put down the itinerary of his visit to the New York Stock Exchange and answered the intercom. 'Why do you ask, Caroline?'

'I'm afraid first class is fully booked and business class can be uncomfortable for anyone much above six-foot-six.'

'Just book a private jet for us both. I'll pay the difference if I have to.'

'Might I suggest we keep it while we're there? It will be cheaper in the long run and you know how poor the legroom is on those awful internal flights. We do have five of them to make in the week we're away.'

The professor sensed an ulterior motive. 'What are you up to now, Mrs Nicholas? Whose birthday is it this time?'

'My nephew's. He wants to be the first in the country to get one of those new *Apals* and they weigh a ton.'

'Apal? The whole purpose of artificial intelligence is to make life easier – your nephew's new plastic friend will be able to board the plane on its own.'

'Oh no! That would make it *second-hand* and you know how fussy children can be.'

Savage tutted at the hold his PA's nephews and nieces appeared to have over her.

He pondered their tour of the US. The ringing of the opening bell at the world's most important trading centre wasn't the main purpose of the journey although the significance of the privilege was. The Americans had taken to the neurologist's treatment for dementia like a duck to water, but it apparently came with some kind of mandatory celebrity obligation so what was originally intended to be a multi-state tour teaching surgery, grew to include a series of radio and television interviews too.

It culminated in the honour of ringing the bell at the start of the world's first trading session controlled by artificial intelligence. The professor had thought about turning it down because he would be so busy instructing but when his hosts realised he owned the company responsible for creating the AI, they became insistent and to the point where Savage thought it rude not to accept.

He looked over the packed programme and tried to work out where to fit in the two hours of sleep he needed each night.

The professor was about to agree to his PA's suggestion when he heard what sounded like a vase crashing to the floor followed by protests and then the noise of a motorised vehicle he knew only too well. The door to his office burst open. Savage raised a hand to acknowledge Caroline's apologies before feigning a welcome to the unannounced visitor.

'Alexandra – what a lovely surprise!'

'Don't you 'lovely' me! Just how many paedophiles are in the ring that runs this place?'

The mildly irritated neurosurgeon walked over to the drinks cabinet. 'Try not to believe every rumour or tittle-tattle of gossip you hear, Ms Salib, it'll only shorten your already limited time on this planet.'

'Don't give me that closed-ranks bollocks, either. How long have you known about the pervert?'

Savage poured himself a drink he didn't bother offering his guest.

'If you're talking about one of this country's finest psychologists, then not much longer than you, judging by the time it took you to get here.'

Alex rammed her chair into one of the many plant pots that decorated his office. 'So, protecting your own? What a surprise. I always knew your sort were made up of every sickness known to mankind.'

The plant appeared vulnerable to a second attack so Savage strode over to protect it. 'Don't you mean 'humankind' or does that particular politically correct noun only apply to *certain* sexes?'

Alex clearly didn't intend spending long in his office. 'If you think I'm going to sit back and watch you protect the monster then you've another thing coming – I've already seen to his replacement and she starts here next week.'

The professor ignored the snub to his involvement in the selection process. 'And Doctor Adams?'

'I don't care – just get rid of him.'

Savage put down his glass and picked up a small bottle. He poured some of what it contained onto a cloth. 'Really Alex, I would have thought being on the brink of *making* government policy and not just carrying it out, you would be the first to recognise an opportunity when you see one especially given our shared ambition for the world.'

'Seeing that disgusting creature commit voluntary euthanasia along with the rest of the scum on your next trial would bring me nothing but pleasure, but even I can see the disquiet that could cause some.'

'So, you finally accept the Alzheimer's patients' thoughts of suicide could actually have been their own?'

'Well, we'll soon find out, won't we? If the majority of your next subjects end up taking advantage of my Euthanasia Bill, then the treatment will be at an end and your reputation with it, but if most start leading healthy lives then the government will continue to support the next stage as expected – either way, I'll be happy.'

'Some of the crimes were unspeakable. It's inevitable one or two will find the gravity of what they did impossible to come to terms with.'

Alex smirked at the hedging of her bets. 'Well, for the sake of the planet and your miserable self, let's hope it's well under half of them.'

The professor wiped the cloth down the leaf of a rubber plant. 'What I meant, with regards to the doctor's clearly unforgivable crime, is that it presents us with an opportunity to reach our goal that much sooner.'

Alex dropped the smiles and manoeuvred her chair closer to him. 'Go on.'

The professor explained it along with how he had ensured James would 'volunteer'.

The corners of Alex's mouth turned back up again.

CHAPTER SEVEN

The doctor half-opened his eyes. For a moment he thought he'd dreamt everything: the clinical trial of the Alzheimer's patients, the selection of the convicts, his arrest, even who he was. James closed his eyes again and tried to remember. Oh yes. One of society's most respected citizens, soon to become one of its most despised.

Someone squeezed his hand.

'Darling? Can you hear me?'

Tracy's voice made him smile. Those few words had everything he needed: love, warmth, compassion, understanding. Even healing – a metaphorical bosom of femininity he could nestle into while forgetting all those nasty masculine thoughts.

James opened his eyes and sat up. He then put a hand to his bandaged head as the mother of all migraines pulsated back and forth across it.

'Whoa! Take it easy. You've only just come out of theatre.' Tracy's hands were joined by someone else's and together they encouraged him back down to the pillows. The pain retreated with James and he looked to see who had assisted her.

A thermometer was inserted into the patient's ear. Savage glanced over at a monitor and grunted approval at the blood pressure returning to normal.

'What's your name?' They both knew the routine well enough.

'Doctor James Edward Adams.'

The thermometer was withdrawn and read. 'Do you know who I am?'

'Professor Sir John Savage.'

'And who are these people?'

James looked at his love and smiled. She smiled back and they squeezed each other's hands. She seemed different somehow. Nothing bad – if anything, the opposite. James put it down to his soporific post-operative recovery and answered the question.

'My future wife and mother of my children, Nurse Tracy Roberts.' Her smile broadened. He wondered why he'd never before noticed how beautiful she was.

James studied the two other people present. He knew the occupant of the wheelchair, but again her appearance had altered, and for the better in some way. He had no idea who the strange hobbit-looking person next to her was, but thought him or her to be just as pleasant. James couldn't put a finger on it but knew his positive attitude had something to do with the desired outcome of the surgery. He wanted to lose his temper but couldn't. He glared at his antagonist. He appeared different too.

'What have you done to me, Professor?' The tone of the question was meant to sound accusatory, but it came out cursory instead.

'Nothing we haven't already discussed at length, James. Your old self will naturally put up a fight for a while, but you know how we fix that.' He used a remote to raise the top third of the bed and held out a small red pill and a beaker of water. 'At least you don't have Alzheimer's or another person in your head to contend with at the same time.'

As a proponent of mental health, James had a good understanding of why the dementia patients suffered from paranoia but never thought he would be able to empathise with them. The fears of his old self felt like seeds that could germinate into something similar if left unchecked so he took what was being offered.

He surveyed the room. 'Everything seems so strange.'

Savage picked up the chart at the end of the bed and made a note.

'I expect a newborn baby would say the same if it were able to.'

Tracy became concerned and drew closer to James. 'Is that what's happened? Is he going to have to relearn everything again like the dementia patients?'

The professor was quick to reassure her. 'No, nothing like that. The treatment's purpose is to enable an ability to view the world differently – an epiphany if you like. Think of it as a meat eater deciding to turn vegetarian, an atheist finding God or vice-versa. Don't worry, Nurse – your fiancé is just how you remember him.' The chart was replaced. 'Only better.'

James sought to placate Tracy about his new

condition. 'Think of it as cognitive behavioural therapy but with guaranteed results.'

Tracy regarded them both with cynicism. 'Well, anything less than perfect and I want him back how he was.'

'You won't be asking for your money back.' Savage picked up an iPad and passed it to James. 'But despite my fabled skill, there's always the chance something was left unplugged during the rewiring process. So let's see, shall we?'

James tapped and swiped through a series of tests. It started with some basic colour and word recognition but soon moved on and up through to the much higher mental processes of reasoning, deduction and knowledge. Before long, he had completed a Mensa test.

Savage checked the result. 'I assume your IQ was less than 170 a few hours ago?' The couple grinned at each other.'

The professor turned to Alex and the hospital's newest psychologist. 'Have you seen enough, ladies?'

Alex encouraged her less physically-impaired colleague to approach the bed. She produced a needle and drove it into the patient.

James stared at it. 'My legs. I can't feel my legs!'

CHAPTER EIGHT

The needle was withdrawn. Tracy and James were beside themselves with grief, and held on to each other for support.

Savage produced a bowl, and placed his phone against James' head. The projectile of vomit only just made it into the container.

The nausea ended as soon as it had started and James grabbed the towel being offered. He wiped it around his mouth. 'What the fuck?'

'Language, James. There are ladies present.' His tormentor removed the bowl and then reached for the iPad. He swiped and tapped it a few times. 'There. Try that.'

James looked at his equally puzzled fiancée and then at his feet. He wiggled his toes before kicking both legs back and forth a couple of times just to make sure. Palpable relief was followed by questions, but they were ignored. Savage turned to Alex and her preferred trial observer and repeated his query.

'Have you seen enough, ladies?'

The merits of a third trial were already being discussed as the women headed for the exit, so he assumed they had. The lab rat's questions restarted the moment the door closed.

One answer was used to cover them all. 'An obvious notion really. I've always found those phone apps that measure things like heart rate to be a bit limiting so thought an upgrade might be appreciated.'

James reeled at the understatement.

'Be serious, Sir John. The science needed to cure paraplegia at the press of a button is a lot more complex than recording one's biometrics. What are you up to this time?'

'There's nothing but altruism behind all my actions, James, although I must admit being the first to establish neural connectivity with a user's smartphone won't do my shares any harm.'

James picked up the iPad. 'You mean I can operate this by thought alone?'

Savage took the tablet from his confused but curious subject and after a few more swipes and taps turned it back towards him. The screen was now black, save for a small white dot in the bottom right-hand corner of it. James was about to take it back when something made him stop. He glanced down to his right, and then back at the professor.

'You're joking, right?'

A cautionary hand was placed on him. 'You've yet to fully recover from your surgery, James. Any problems, just move your eyes rapidly in any direction and you'll come out of *augmented* consciousness.'

James stared at the white dot in his field of view.

The home page of the hospital's website filled the room in front of him. He moved his head around. The page stayed where it was. He thought of one of the menu items and a new page appeared. Before long, James had been right through what the site had to offer. Tracy looked at her fiancé staring straight ahead and then at what he was doing on the iPad.

James was impressed. 'This is incredible. It's going to revolutionise the way we do,' he stopped and moved his eyes as instructed, 'everything.'

He wiggled his toes again. 'You deliberately paralysed my legs, didn't you?'

The professor half-turned his head towards the door. 'As I've said previously, Ms Salib is keen to discover exactly what the treatment is capable of. However, her increasing popularity with the public means she's likely to be highly influential when it comes to society's acceptance of the more sensitive capabilities and I'm afraid that has a personal agenda.'

Tracy interjected. 'But she must know she'll never actually be able to use her legs. She's had the condition since childhood – they're too underdeveloped.'

'Who knows what you women are thinking?' Savage stood up. 'Not that I anticipate such an inability to be an issue for long.' He gestured towards the iPad. 'Not once the whole world has access to each other's thoughts.'

CHAPTER NINE

'See if you can do it with one hand this time.'

James had to grit his teeth, but soon had another coin torn apart.

Bits of bent and rent change lay in his lap. 'That's amazing.' Tracy wrapped her hands around one of his biceps and mocked idolatry. 'My hero!'

James half-scoffed. 'It's not only about strength.' He picked up one half of the ten-pence piece he'd just made impossible to use as currency. 'The alloy becomes hot – its molecular structure must alter in some way to assist the process.' He brought the damaged side of the remnant up close to one eye. 'It's as if it's being made to tear by *psychological* as well as physical means. Willpower if you like.' He dropped it.

'Darling, are you alright?'

The doctor looked around the room and then back at Tracy. 'I can see…' He focussed on one of her diamond ear studs and zoomed into it until the individual flaws of the gem were obvious. ' Everything.'

Tracy put her arms across her chest. James laughed.

'Don't worry, darling, I don't have X-ray vision.' He raised a hand to his face and glanced at both sides of it.

'Sadly.' He dropped his arm back to the bed and stared straight ahead.

'I'm beginning to understand what an "epiphany" really means. The Professor hasn't just enabled the mind to think differently – the way it controls the body has changed too.' He picked up one of the metal shards from his lap and threw it towards a waste bin. It fell into the centre of it. He did the same with the other half but made it bounce off two surfaces first.

He selected another and looked at Tracy. 'The question is, is this a good thing or a bad thing?' The partly-damaged disc of metal struck the top of a table and two walls before clinking against the previous projectiles – and all while his eyes remained fixed on the most beautiful woman he had ever seen.

Tracy took hold of his hand and spoke slowly. 'Darling. If Sir John *has* improved everything about you, does that mean…' She nodded in a particular direction – *'Everything?'*

'I volunteered hoping the treatment would suppress that side of my nature, Tracy not encourage it.'

'Typical of a man to think I was talking about sex – I meant our children. Will they be *improved* too?'

'Of course!' Savage had entered the room. 'But why leave things to chance?'

He tapped and swiped away at the iPad he now appeared to have permanent possession of. It was then turned towards Tracy. There were two cartoon-like images on the screen – one was of a baby girl, the other a boy.

The professor tapped the picture of the girl and a menu appeared. 'My engineers tell me it's in beta, but I still think what they've achieved is remarkable.' The tablet was offered to her.

Tracy kept her distance while viewing the selections available. Starting with the number of female ova a mother might wish to have growing inside her, the other options extended to literally thousands judging by the length of the scrollbar. Tracy extended a finger and tentatively selected 'Eyes'. The sub-menu that appeared made it clear more than just colour was available: size, shape, distance between – every possible permutation could be factored in and all at the press of a button. There was even a 'preview' which showed how the child could be expected to look not just at birth, but at every age from then on – all the way to her predicted death by some kind of unforeseen domestic accident at the age of 228.

Tracy appeared both fascinated and disturbed. She stood back with a shake of her head.

'What's the meaning of this, Professor?' The fledgling nature of James' condition ensured the statement came out with all the gravitas of the newborn *he* was.

'Like the Alzheimer's patients, I'm afraid it's going to take the red pill a while to blend the old James Adams with the new, so an initial inability to appreciate all the treatment's benefits is understandable.'

'Benefits? You call the deliberate interference of a child's natural development, a 'benefit'?'

'So, to be absolutely clear about this James. You would be perfectly happy to see your mutated genes passed on and down through Nurse Robert's lineage?'

Tracy's concerns switched to the health of her future husband's sperm. 'Why? What has he got?'

The traits were brought up on the iPad and read out along with the probability of their children inheriting them. 'Cystic fibrosis: 25%; Huntington's: 50%; Tumours: 50%.' Savage peered over the top of the screen. 'The inability to see common sense: 100%.'

Tracy grimaced at her now, sheepish partner. 'And just when were you going to tell me about all those? I don't want our children anywhere near them!'

James relented. 'Okay, okay. So I might be persuaded by the 'benefits' of eradicating inherited diseases but there's absolutely no way we're choosing the sex, let alone the colour of their eyes.'

Savage put the tablet down. 'Really? Tell me, Ms Roberts, how many children do you plan on having?'

Tracy's eyes darted between the two men. 'Er, well, two boys and a girl would be nice.' Her other half concurred.

'And I sincerely hope you get your wish but supposing the boys come along first? Would you actually turn down the chance of *guaranteeing* what you long for? What if the family were then blessed with a third boy? Would you honestly refuse the opportunity again? And again after that? No significant discovery or invention was ever ignored for the sake of some ethical or moral objection and I put it to you that if it were at all possible to ensure the safest and most desirable outcome, you would willingly seize it.'

Tracy looked at James as if expecting him to make the decision. He sighed. 'Okay, Sir John. The situation's clearly a good deal more complicated than I'd given it credit.' He pointed at the iPad. 'But *designer* children? *Really?*'

The professor picked it up. 'No. Not really. A bit like turning the dementia patients from pacifists to Nazis and vice versa, I can't resist pushing the science to its logical extremes.' He smiled at the two of them. 'Told you I needed someone to keep an eye on me.'

CHAPTER TEN

Professor Savage stood alone in the Oval Office. Quite the ending to his arrival in America.

The flight had been diverted to Washington DC minutes before the scheduled touchdown at JFK and just over an hour later a helicopter deposited both him and his PA onto the lawns of the White House. Caroline thought it all very *West Wing* and jumped at the chance of an impromptu tour of the President's official residence. Her boss kept his cynicism a little more intact and knew more than good ol' southern hospitality lay behind the gentle hijacking of his busy schedule. The level of interest in his visit was still nonetheless intriguing and he wondered if the nation's first President 'born 'n' raised' in Alabama would prove to be as charming as his television chat-show-host persona made him out to be.

Savage looked through one of the windows to admire the blossom on the crab-apple trees.

'Beaut' ain't they?'

The professor turned around and did something rare for him – tilted his head *up* to see a face. 'Mr President – how do you do. John Savage. I do apologise, I didn't quite catch what you said?'

The hand that grasped his was in keeping with the rest of the body – huge. The nation's leader was at least seven-feet tall. Savage already knew that of course but seeing President Donald J Kalten in the flesh was an experience in itself – a broad smile no doubt engendered to make the moment less intimidating did the exact opposite as the professor found himself being pulled towards it.

'Don't speak 'inglish, don't speak 'merican, 'a-speak bammy.' He burst out laughing and pushed his somewhat relieved detainee away again. 'Just joshin' wid ya, Johnny boy – 'a can speak what you people call *The Queen's* English just as good as any Brit.' He walked over to the famous desk and picked up the bottle of Macallan the professor had spied the moment he was shown into the President's office. 'For example – 'a do believe the polite reply to your greetin', 'how do you do' is to repeat back the exact same phrase – 'cos it's not a question – it's a formality.' He uncorked the whisky and began pouring it. 'Am 'a right?'

Savage smiled as he nodded.

'Course, there's a downside to speakin' right and I get it every time 'a talk to ma' maw and paw on the phone or go back to ma' home town of Daleville – 'a try real-hard to sound like 'a used to but they always tell me 'as changed and as proud of their boy as 'a know they is 'a can sense the disappointment in their voices.' He picked up the two glasses and walked over to his enforced guest. 'Have you ever disappointed someone close to you, Johnny?' The professor hoped what lay behind his kidnap was about to be explained.

He motioned to take one of the glasses but the President withdrew them both before gesturing towards the couch.

'Have a seat.'

Savage sat down.

'Here's ta' honesty.' Both men raised their glasses to that.

The liquid had barely reached the professor's lips when he sensed it had been spiked with something. He analysed what it was while giving the appearance of savouring the 100-year malt. The chemical composition was a sedative of some kind but synthesised to ensure the absence of colour, odour and taste. He calculated it had been designed to leave him unconscious for around thirty minutes – more than enough time for someone to give him a physical examination. Savage metabolised the contaminant into something benign and decided to go along with whatever his less-than-genuine host's intentions were.

Kalten shook him a couple of times, and then called in the team of doctors and scientists he had standing by. It wasn't long before they'd made a record and taken the samples needed. Savage could have disconnected his pain receptors as the various needles went in, but with eyes closed, all remaining senses were required to make records of his own. He reduced their sensitivity instead. The removal of a sample of sperm was still uncomfortable, though – in more ways than one.

It ended with the completion of where they had started – a photographic record of what became visible when parting the hair on the professor's head. They clearly had good reason to think he'd undergone the same procedure as the Alzheimer's patients and Savage wondered where that interest came from. His patience was rewarded with the answer.

The President looked at his experts. 'Well?'

'He's definitely undergone the same surgery, and around the time our German friend was still alive judging by the age of the scars.' The scientist lifted a small case. 'We'll get these analysed but I'm sure they'll confirm it.'

Kalten sat down. 'So it's true. That son-of-a-bitch Nazi doctor did more than beef up our cattle and men – the British were involved too.' The President went to take a sip of his whisky but thought better of it. 'He even taught the professor here everything he knew. The question is, how has that been developed over the last sixty years? There's got to be more to it than fixin' has-beens or ped-o-files.' He stood up. 'How do we know he's not *pretendin'* to be asleep? How do we know he's not listenin' to everythin' we're saying right now?'

'It's possible.' Their captive's hair was parted again. 'Doctor Mengele's remit was to improve strength and endurance but it looks as if the British utilised the *full* extent of his discoveries.' Savage was starting to enjoy the conversation.

'Which explains why am' the size of a house but dumb as a bag of hammers. Okay – let's wake up the Aryan genius.'

The professor was relieved to sense something that

amounted to nothing more than smelling salts. He didn't need to act the effect of them.

The President still seemed keen on theatrics, though. 'Oh ma gawsh, Johnny – are you okay? One sip an' you passed right-out. Mebbe it's not such a good idea to drink Scotch straight after a long flight?'

'That's quite alright, Mr President. Single malt whisky is my weakness I'm afraid.' He teased his newest adversary by reaching for the glass again. It couldn't have been pushed out of his reach any faster.

'Nope, 'a don't think that would be wise given the circumstances. Let me get you a cup-a-coffee instead.' He looked at the departing medical advisors. 'Gentlemen, Sir John and I are mi-dee grateful for your assistance – 'a wonder if you could arrange that an' sen' in the Secretary of State and her team at the same time?'

Despite his host's insincerity, Savage quite liked him. He'd certainly like to get him on an operating table to see what the Americans had actually managed to achieve in the field of eugenics.

A stern-looking group of political and military advisors arrived along with the promised coffee and a tray of sandwiches. The President picked up half of them in one grab and made the introductions. He then feigned ignorance about the purpose of it all.

'Excuse my being a dumb-ass, Johnny, but these boys 'n' girls would like to ask you some questions and as 'am just a hick from Backwardsville without a hope in hell of understandin' most of 'em, I'll just sit in this 'ere chair and mind ma' own – holler if anything starts treading on the toes of that gracious Queen o' yours and I'll put 'em right back in their box.' The sandwiches didn't stay in his hand for long.

Savage liked his host even more. There was something innately clever about the self-awareness of ignorance, and the man's ability to compensate for that with the knowledge and skills of others – certainly less intrusive than his solution.

The professor turned to his inquisitors. 'Good morning. And how may I be of assistance to the world's greatest democracy?'

The Chief of Staff spoke first. 'Excuse the direct approach, Sir John, but we're concerned your visit may involve you having to answer questions that could cause embarrassment to our respective governments. Do you mind answering them here first?'

'Of course not. Anything to help break down barriers so that the benefits of my work can be enjoyed by all.'

The Secretary of State interrupted. 'That's exactly what we're afraid of, Sir John. We're already aware your treatment has far greater potential than the mere healing of the sick or curing of the sexually insane and we'd rather the world didn't find that out on Saturday night television.'

The attempt to uncover the extent of the professor's work was pitiful but unsurprising. 'Madame Secretary, it won't surprise you to learn the British government shares the exact same concern which is why the treatment's development is carefully scrutinised and controlled by a cross-party committee at every step.'

The SoS was about to pass her opinion on that when she was interrupted by her cigarette-rolling President. 'Well, 'scuse ma' French but that's just horseshit.' He licked the paper to seal in the tobacco and stood up. 'Leavin' sumthin' as important as the security o' this great nation to a dyke commie in a wheelchair is about as sensible as a bucket o' babies.' He looked at the senior military man present as if to get to the point of the meeting. The general did.

'The thing is, Sir John, you don't need me to tell you we're at war – with Islamic fundamentalism. It's only a matter of time before there's another US-led invasion, and our brave boys and girls need to be at their peak when that happens.' He glanced at his President. 'Now, we already have the muscle; what we're missing are the brains.' Savage thought that *very* profound.

The general pointed at their captive. 'You weren't born a genius – you were made one and if that can be taught to our surgeons you'd be performing a great service to the free world.'

The professor stood up. 'Ladies and gentlemen. I've listened to what you have to say and been genuinely moved.' He spotted a bust of Winston Churchill and strode over to it. 'And just as Uncle Sam came to the aid of John Bull in his hour of need, then so shall John Savage return the honour.' He turned to face his plainly suspicious but still needy interrogators. 'My knowledge and skills are at the disposal of your finest neurosurgeons and it gives me the greatest of pleasure and pride to say that they will soon be providing what you require.' He beamed at his host. 'You won't be disappointed with the results, Mr President.'

The stereotypical southerner lit the roll-up. He then gestured towards his various advisors. 'They all thought ya' wuz some stiff Brit that needed a rocket up yer ass, but 'a knew as soon as 'a looked into them big ol' blue-eyes of yours that you were a good 'un.' He pressed a button on the desk and the door was opened by a Marine sergeant. 'Yer' free to go – er, 'a mean, enjoy the rest of yer stay in our beautiful country.' The menacing grin made a reappearance. 'It's been a pleasure – 'am sure we'll meet again someday.'

Savage paused to allow someone the chance to remember the gift of an untampered 100-year bottle of Scotch but when the silence began turning awkward, decided to leave empty-handed instead.

The door had no sooner closed than the US military's most senior officer voiced his concerns but Kalten had no such qualms.

'D'ya know what the Briddish fear most, General? Looking tough. They're afraid the moment they rattle a sword or stamp a foot in some negotiation, accusations of colonial imperialism will come back to haunt them.' He looked out of the window. 'It's their way of coming to terms with losing the world's greatest empire. You'd think a country that once ruled a third of the Earth's surface and spawned its greatest democracy back in 1776 would be proud of their achievements, but no, they'd much rather dwell on the guilt of having killed and enslaved a few niggers, raped women and stolen their resources. The result? An all but official government policy of atonement that champions the weak at the expense of the strong.'

He pointed out the manicured trees and plants in the Rose garden. 'If the Brits had their way, that garden would be made *fairer* with inferior species an' weeds allowed to compete *equally* with the beautiful specimens our horticulturalists spent decades perfectin'.'

Kalten turned to the advisors. 'So while they continue to appease their guilt by applyin' the treatment to the *least* productive in their society, we'll be selecting the *most* deservin' in ours.' He took a puff of his cigarette. 'An' in the process, creatin' the greatest race of people the world has ever seen.'

CHAPTER ELEVEN

James tutted at his inability to view anything other than the hospital's internal website. Use of the internet was possible – just not by this particular method of access. Surfing the web hands-free would eventually be allowed however, as each application or function he thought about presented him with a timer. The period remaining varied between each, which indicated the professor planned a gradual introduction to James' more advanced capabilities. Much to his frustration, the first of those was still at least three months away. He flitted his eyes left and right a few times, picked up the tablet and accessed the internet conventionally.

Although a week had passed and James was now up and about again, his condition still felt strange and the few new capabilities he could exercise did little to ease what was fast becoming his biggest problem – boredom. The party tricks with the coins had long since worn out their novelty, and learning a new language or completing *The Times* crossword in a few minutes, just as banal.

In fact, James spent most of his waking hours trying to work out not what the professor had improved about him but what had been changed or even removed. The replacement psychologist had assessed him using the tests James himself had designed for the volunteers, but what Tracy and he had discovered about the Alzheimer's trial still plagued his waking hours, so James decided to take some broader personality tests too. As a psychological tool, they were blunt but appeared to indicate he was still the stable extrovert he always was, not to mention the same reluctant Tory voter. A couple of the results implied less arrogance than before but as others demonstrated an improvement in confidence James put that down to differing author interpretations – a bit like one person's freedom fighter being another's terrorist.

James thought his use of the word 'person's' as opposed to 'man's' freedom fighter was interesting and was about to investigate that when the door opened.

'And how's my brave soldier?' James lost his train of thought. He got out of bed and rushed over to hold the visitor close.

'Have I ever told you how much I love you?'

'More in the last seven days than in the entire time we've known each other.'

James sensed an element of irritation in the reply. He stepped back from her.

'Sorry darling, the last thing I want to do is suffocate you with my feelings.'

Tracy pulled him close again. 'It's not that – I love you just as much and always will, but you can have too much of a good thing and much as I like chocolate, the thought of eating it for breakfast, lunch and dinner every day makes me feel sick.'

James' concern turned to hurt. 'Are you saying you're sick of me?'

'Darling, no, of course not. I love you more than ever, but I think it's going to take us *both* a while to get used to the new you.'

He studied her face. Her beauty was intoxicating. James had to close his eyes to ask his next question. 'You mean I'm different now in more ways than just an improved IQ and my ability to tear a copy of the city's telephone directory in half?'

'God, yes and all for the better – I've never known you to be so attentive and understanding of my feelings and needs.' Tracy glanced at the bed. 'What happened last night after I managed to get us some privacy was proof of that.'

James relaxed and mocked his hurt this time. 'Are you trying to tell me I was rubbish in bed before?'

Tracy laughed. 'No, far from it. But it was all a bit 'wham-bam, thank-you-ma'am' and much as a girl enjoys that, it's nice to think her man's there just for her sometimes and now you are.'

James pondered that thought. He had assumed an ability to satisfy his fiancée in every way came with what the professor insisted was an ability to *see* things differently, but he did wonder if at least some of that hadn't been engineered for a reason.

She took the iPad from him.

'Do you mind? I'm doing some vital psychological research.'

Tracy ignored his protests. 'And I want to see how the

professor's guest appearance on *The Late Show* went last night.' James relented and sat down with her to watch it.

They both started chuckling the moment they saw how the programme's producer had decided to introduce him. The show's determination to be as entertaining as possible usually began with some kind of parody skit at the expense of the hapless guest's dignity, and this was no exception – the world's most respected neurosurgeon was dressed as Hollywood's version of Mary Shelley's most famous character with the compere of the show playing his sidekick, Igor. The studio was decorated with props placed to make it appear like *Frankenstein's* laboratory and a 'monster' lay on a table in the middle of it. The jokes were predictably lame but that didn't bother Tracy and James – the look of utter bewilderment on their boss's face provided all the entertainment they needed. To the professor's palpable relief, the skit ended, and an armchair interview began.

The compere reminded the studio audience of how important their guest was. The standing ovation to show the country's appreciation of the 'cure' for dementia was the only genuine part of the programme and Savage acknowledged the recognition with a slight bow.

'So, come on, Professor – tell us what else you've got brewing in that laboratory of yours?' Savage didn't get a chance to answer as the compere then turned to bait the audience. 'We wanna see some *real* monsters don't we?' Their response was enthusiastic.

Savage was clearly uncomfortable with the show's format but tried his best. 'Well, I'm not sure about *monsters.*' The audience tittered but Tracy and James listened intently. 'But I can promise something perhaps more intriguing in the not too distant future.' The studio became quiet. 'Imagine waking up one morning with the ability to do *anything*. Climb Mount Everest or go to the Moon? You can. Be the President of the United States or score the winning touchdown in the last second of the Super Bowl? You can.' He emphasised the extent of the possibilities. 'Or how about being a *super* athlete, soldier or hero? You can.' It sounded inevitable. 'Very soon we'll all be able to do absolutely *anything*.'

A period of silence was followed by an attempt to burst what appeared to be the professor's bubble. 'I hate to be the first to break the news to you, Professor, but while you've been busy with test tubes the rest of us have been doing that with Virtual Reality.'

Savage gave his host a look as if he were being likened to a man that still used a typewriter. '*Virtual* Reality? Those clumsy, sick-making devices? I'm talking about *Real* Reality.'

The compere recovered his animated persona. 'Real Reality? I'll tell you what's *real*, Professor – my wife. She won't even let me *watch* the Super Bowl let alone play in it.' The audience dutifully responded and the show regained its frenetic pace.

'Whatever, Professor, as long as it doesn't involve making any *holes* in me, I'm happy.' The compere turned to the audience again. 'Because I need a hole in the head – like a hole in the head!' The *YouTube* clip ended as the canned laughter started.

'Well, he's right. Being able to do all that stuff is one thing, but finding the time quite another.' Tracy handed the tablet back. 'And you're going to be busy providing for a family.'

James dismissed her interpretation. 'There's nothing *real* about it – the Professor was referring to what the treatment will enable our minds to more realistically imagine – we can't all be President.'

Tracy grabbed the tablet and shook it at him. 'Well, if it involves you staring into space all day with this on your lap – forget it.'

James grimaced at her. He read between the professor's lines. 'It's what he *didn't* say which was more interesting. Why not mention what the treatment can do for the disabled? The Professor would have received a second standing ovation if he had explained nearly all mental and physical abnormalities will soon be just as much a thing of the past as dementia.'

'The Professor's made no secret of the fact he wants *everyone* to benefit from the treatment, James. What he said just fitted in with that.'

James was about to respond when he stood up, strode over to Tracy and grabbed her by both arms. 'If you were trying to make the world a better place and knew that the way to do it was to get everyone to see things differently through surgery – how would you convince them to go through with it?' He placed a finger on her lips. 'Bear in mind you've just witnessed the pleasing and yet at the same time unsettling sight of prisons closing because the inmates were all made to think *correctly*.'

Tracy gave that some thought. 'If the treatment's going to be seen as more than a cure for the sick, lame and lazy, then there would have to be one hell of an incentive for all of society to volunteer for brainwashing.'

'Exactly! And what better way than to make people think they would be *inferior* without it? James gathered her up into his arms and leapt onto the bed. 'Once society is aware of how I and others can not only pleasure in ways not thought possible but both metaphorically and literally kick trains off tracks and leap tall buildings in a single bound, how long do you think it's going be before brainwashing is not only accepted but *demanded*?'

Tracy looked at her Superman. 'Not long at all – you can let go of me now.' James apologised and lowered his Lois Lane back to the floor. She walked over to the door and turned the key in it.

James lay back on the bed and looked up at the ceiling. 'I wonder what my old self would have to say about it?'

Tracy wandered back and began undoing the buttons to her blouse. 'I don't know. But I want this self to fuck me.'

CHAPTER TWELVE

Alex wallowed in the pain-free bliss of an orgasm. She had no idea how long it would last and didn't particularly care – she just knew that right now she was in Heaven. If only that could be made permanent in some way.

The cannabis joint that would be required upon her return was prepared. Sunita had satisfied Alex enough in the past to know the exact moment and lit the spliff before drawing from it herself. She kissed her idol and then replaced her lips with the MP's second-most favoured method of temporary pain control. Alex tried to get the marijuana to mimic the impact of her preferred choice but to no avail. The less-effective but nonetheless just-as-welcome painkiller began its work and she half-opened her eyes.

Alex looked at the emotion in the person that stared back. Even in her most blissful state, Alex couldn't return it. She didn't love Sunita. Never had and never would. Alex had never loved anyone. Not even her own mother.

It was pointless getting close to someone – they would soon leave you. Alex knew that cynicism stemmed from being abandoned by her father as a child but was only two at the time so her recollections were hardly accurate let alone objective. The change in her mother was real enough, though.

It couldn't have been easy on either parent when their child was born little more than a malformed foetus. Alex should have died but thanks to the dedication of a medical team, one of the world's most premature and impaired births managed to survive. It was all down to advances in biomedical science of course – if her parents had met as little as two years previously Alex would now be some curious oddity in a specimen jar. Her distinct and unusual visual deformities would have seen to that.

In some quarters, Alex's survival could be viewed as a miracle from God, but when the day-to-day realities of what that meant for her parents became evident, something had to give and despite daily support from both medical and social services, her father decided it was all too much for him and he left.

Alex only had her mother's version of these events to go on of course. For all she knew, her father could have abandoned them because he couldn't stand his partner's abuse of the bottle. That was certainly how Alex viewed her mother's 'love'.

Her mother must have at least tried to love her daughter in the months and years that followed, but a decision to commit to alcohol instead made Alex increasingly seek the sober but less personal company of her carers. The combination of that and a chronic condition meant any normal mother/daughter relationship was all but impossible, with many a fraught row and words later regretted. As a teenager, Alex couldn't wait to get away so by the time university came around, entering the semi-independent world came more as relief, rather than the mixture of trepidation and excitement it should have been.

The last thing Alex could remember her mother saying before she committed suicide was, 'If only you had been different.'

Sunita appeared to mistake the tear that ran out of her lover's eye as reciprocation. 'I love you, too.' She kissed Alex passionately but there was no response. She offered the joint again. That was refused too.

'Suni, would you do *anything* for me?'

The response implied it was a ridiculous question. 'Of course, I would – even if I didn't love you, who could refuse a future Prime Minister?'

'There's a lot to be done should that ever happen and I'm going to need people I can rely on.'

Sunita was aware of her limitations. 'I'm not exactly the cleverest person in the world, Al, and I know absolutely nothing about politics. I didn't even go to university. What possible use could I be?' She grinned. 'Apart from the obvious.'

'Sometimes, commitment to a cause is more important than knowledge of it and I need someone to be there for me when the time comes.'

'Use and abuse my body as you wish, Al. You know I would do anything for you.'

'Including walking again?'

Sunita leaned away. 'You mean?'

Alex nodded and then tried to ignore the pain

her lover's hugs caused. Sunita let go and apologised. Another puff was encouraged as compensation.

Sunita looked at her useless legs. 'I can't believe it! What's changed your mind? I thought you said Savage was a monster who just wanted to turn society into slaves for the rich?'

Alex waited for her pain to subside again before replying. 'He is, and does. But as I've said before, you have to get close to a monster before you can kill it and I'm going to need legs to carry me there.' Sunita appeared puzzled. 'Don't worry, Suni – it's just a figure of speech.' Alex closed her eyes again as the full effect of the weed washed over her once more. 'You'll be joining a group of other impaired sisters as soon as the current trial is over.'

Sunita grimaced at the mention of the treatment's present-day beneficiaries. 'Ugh! *Men*. I don't know why you chose the inferior sex over us – especially such disgusting examples.'

'I needed to ensure the suicidal thoughts of the dementia sufferers were particular to them and that appears to be the case.' She smiled. 'But you'll be pleased to hear the realisation of what the paedoes did is likely to cause at least some to take advantage of my new Act when it becomes law.'

They kissed again but then Sunita broke away. 'What if the treatment makes me think differently too?' She fretted. 'What if *I* want to commit suicide?!'

'You won't. Apparently there has to be a 'logical' reason so you'd better tell me now if you've done something you're likely to regret enough to want to take your own life.'

Sunita thought carefully. 'Taking someone's school dinner money after I left mine at home?'

'Then I guess you're going to hell in a handcart.'

CHAPTER THIRTEEN

'Doctor Frankenstein, I presume?'

'Very droll, Tarquin – get me a stiff drink. I need one. Eight hours on a return flight listening to an Apal going through its set-up procedure has just about finished me off.'

The Business Secretary had already anticipated the need, and passed him a glass. 'Yes, I've heard about these new companion toys for children and how they're a prelude to a whole host of labour-saving devices. I assume owning one of the few companies that makes them helped sugar the experience.' Tarquin presented Savage with the business section of *The Times*. 'I'm certainly enjoying what my shares have been doing since you rang the bell this morning.'

Savage looked at the prices and then at his smartphone to see what the market had done since. He turned it towards the Asquith-Bennington's most promising son.

'Got to hand it to you, John. You know business almost as well as you know the human brain. If half the guff you promise comes to pass, we can just about rule the world.'

'*We?*'

Tarquin guided him in search of somewhere quieter.

He talked as they walked. 'The thing is John, it's common knowledge the PM intends standing down before the next general election and much as I hate the thought of parading myself with the rest of the degrading flesh that masquerades as a selection process, I've decided to throw my hat in.' They sat down in a secluded corner of the club. 'Now, thanks to my business policies, this country has never been in a better position to invest in its people.' He leaned in closer. 'I've developed a plan which not only puts the finances back in the black over the next five years but by 2035, the average family won't be paying a penny in tax either.' Tarquin's sense of self-satisfaction was all too evident. 'And once my family has helped the blue-rinse brigade that runs this party make their decision, I'll be all but guaranteed the leadership.'

Savage regarded his friend with cynicism. 'Allow me to put a different spin on things. Thanks to the export success of the treatment, revenue from the worldwide eradication of crime, insanity and nearly all physical impairments, means this country need never want for cash again. Naturally, as the Secretary of State for Business, your paymasters will know that happened on your watch.' He acknowledged the credibility of Tarquin's ambitions. 'Throw in the good fortunes of timing and parentage, and I fail to see what further assistance I can provide.'

Tarquin sighed. 'Despite that great success, John, I'm afraid the pollsters tell us a healthy majority at the next general election is still far from assured. I know it's hard to believe but there's an increasingly ungrateful part of the population that views us with suspicion, and all because they couldn't afford to attend the same school. These people could be gifted with all the cash, hospitals and colleges ever needed and they'd still vote for a corduroy-jacket wearing relic from the Eighties simply because he's 'nice'.'

Savage studied his glass. 'Well, that's the trouble with our sort, Tarquin. We insist incest is the answer to political perfection without realising that doesn't just produce small chins and big noses but a sense of entitlement that only succeeds in provoking the less well-connected.' He offered a second reason for the Socialist's apparent ungratefulness. 'It's always fascinated me how the left despises the right but the worst that can be mustered in return is a sneer or occasionally, pity. Both end in incensing the Marxists further. I guess that's why we're known as, 'The nasty party'.'

'Yes, but you can do something about that.' Tarquin checked the surroundings. 'How did your meeting go with the President?'

Savage fell silent. Despite the controlled release of information, he did wonder how much the government knew of his work. The question indicated he needed to explore the extent of it. 'Why don't you tell me?'

Tarquin put a hand on his friend's knee. 'There's no need to be modest. I know you promised to turn his GIs into thinking robots as well as muscle machines. I just want you to do the same for this country – that's all.'

'It's easy to promise something that comes with the

treatment anyway – IQ increases by at least thirty basis points, regardless.'

'I said, don't be modest, John. We both know what's possible. Your disgraced psychologist's decision to raise his concerns directly was most insightful.'

The professor became silent again.

His oldest so-called friend tried sounding reasonable. 'Look. I'm not asking for a nation of Thatcherites let alone Nazis, I just want to ensure at least 50% of voters put a cross next to our party on polling day – that's all.' Tarquin likened it to something just as immoral but less unsettling. 'Think of it as subliminal advertising. If kids can be made to demand an Apal each for Christmas or a bunch of geriatrics to commit suicide, then encouraging more than 50% of the population to vote *correctly* should be a walk in the park'.

'The election is only a year away. Assuming it's decided the procedure is safe for all at the end of the current trial, you'll be lucky if even 10% of the population have been treated by then let alone 'understand' what's required of them.'

'Ah yes, but when people realise they won't just be clever but stronger and fitter too, everyone will be beating a path to your and every other brain surgeon's door especially as it will soon be available on the NHS. Granted, the *whole* population won't be in a position to see the light, but I'm sure if we concentrate on a few left-leaning types, the percentage needed for an electoral majority will cease to be an issue.' Tarquin sat back and gazed into the bottom of his glass. 'Of course, this would all become academic if the public were accidentally to find out paedophiles not only partook in the current trial but, unfortunately, exist amongst the staff too.'

The professor looked at the corner of the bar he'd apparently been backed into. He raised his glass. 'Here's to the next Prime Minister!'

CHAPTER FOURTEEN

The barrister referred to his notes. 'Well, the good news, if one can call it that, is your computer contained just under 5,000 *legal* pornographic images.'

James hung his head at the shame of it all. Savage remained impassive.

'The bad news is, a further 452 are deemed to be *illegal*.'

'How many?' James was both stunned and horrified by the figure.

'But that's not the *really* bad news. Of those, 149 are considered to be at the highest category of child abuse imagery – rape and torture. And it's those that will send you to prison.'

James couldn't take it all in. 'But I haven't seen *one* illegal image let alone *hundreds*.'

The QC closed the file and placed it back on the table. 'Computer forensics is pretty much an exact science these days I'm afraid – they're definitely there. There's no mistake.'

The figures were academic. James had already resigned himself. 'What am I looking at?'

'The maximum is five years. Assuming you plead

guilty at the first opportunity and the judge accepts the professor's treatment as mitigation then that could be reduced to two.' The gravity of the situation was made clear. 'It doesn't matter that it's a first offence or you've never physically harmed a child – the law says possession of images encourages sexual abuse and the penalty for that is punitive.' The QC exchanged looks with Savage. 'I recommend you plead *not* guilty.'

James jerked his head up. 'What do you mean?'

The barrister tapped the file. 'There's no proof of what you did.'

'Of course there is – it's on my laptop.'

'It might be on your computer but that doesn't mean you were responsible for the images on it.'

'Are you asking me to lie in court?'

'No, of course not, but you just told me you've not seen the images you're accused of. If you genuinely believe that, then you should plead not guilty.'

The doctor looked at both men in disbelief. 'Do you really think society cares whether there are ten, ten-thousand or ten-million images? Just one is enough to convince people there's no smoke without fire and I probably raped or have even *killed* children.'

'Then all the more reason to plead not guilty. You didn't pay or ask for the images so other than the pictures themselves, the Crown Prosecution Service doesn't have the evidence they need to secure a conviction. If you plead not guilty they would have to rely on arguments in court which will almost certainly lead to the acceptance of fewer images and a comparable reduction in your sentence.'

'To what?'

'Maybe a year.'

James laughed. 'Gentlemen. Hardly a day goes by without at least one of the tabloids exaggerating something to do with paedophilia, especially if an establishment figure like me can be tied to it. I'm ashamed enough without a 'not guilty' plea prolonging the case just so my sentence can be reduced by a single year – I'm amazed the papers haven't picked up on it already.' He clarified his original intention. 'No, I don't care if I get the full five years. I'm pleading guilty in the hope they'll be something more newsworthy on the day. Whatever shape my life takes after I come out of prison, the less people know about it, the better.'

The two older men exchanged raised eyebrows before the QC stood up and put the file back into his briefcase. 'If you plead guilty to something you didn't do then justice will not have been served and that cannot be right. It puts me in a very difficult position and if it wasn't for Sir John, I would probably refuse to take your case.'

James was frustrated. 'Justice? You need to get out of these chambers more often. Whatever I plead in court, *justice* is the last thing that will have been done.' He pointed out of the window. '*That's* where I'll be judged and for the rest of my life.'

The barrister made some parting comments James didn't listen to and left the room. Savage got to his feet. 'If it's any consolation, James I admire your stance. By pleading guilty at the outset you not only reduce your own chances of being splashed across the front pages of the red-tops but mine and the hospital's too and for that, I'm grateful.'

James had accepted the inevitable. 'I'm sorry, Sir John. I appreciate the opportunity of the treatment and your reasoning behind it but it looks as if my life is over anyway.' He became contrite. 'I apologise for thinking there was some kind of malicious intent behind everything you do.' James became awkward too. 'And I'm sorry if the concerns I raised directly with the Health Secretary have caused you some difficulties.'

The professor placed a hand on his ex-colleague's shoulder. 'That's quite alright, old chap – no harm done. We both did what we thought was right.' He hesitated. 'Of course, I and others would understand if you decide to take the honourable way out to save everyone's blushes.'

James looked up. 'Yes, that's the *perfect* solution. I can't think why I worried about it before. It solves everything – by taking advantage of the new voluntary euthanasia law, my case will have to be dropped and the hospital and you can carry on as if nothing happened.' He became sad. 'Tracy will have to come with me, of course.'

CHAPTER FIFTEEN

'What *am* I talking about?' James turned to the professor. 'Why does it feel natural to me that Tracy should want to commit suicide too?' Once again, his question sounded more like an apology for impertinence as opposed to any serious inquiry into his mental state.

The response put his new mind to rest. 'It's just the treatment, James. You love each other and plan to spend your lives together so it's only natural you should want to die as a couple too. Don't worry, once Tracy's had the operation, she'll be equally enthusiastic although I wouldn't advise informing her of your decision before then.'

James agreed. He looked at the professor's iPad. 'I wonder what my previous self would have to say on the matter?'

The tablet was switched on. 'I don't know. Shall we find out?'

'How?'

'By reverting back to your previous personality of course. The brain's no different to any other computer – changes can be undone if required.' The tablet woke up and Savage tapped the screen. 'But I don't know many who've decided to go back to *Windows Ten* no matter how much they missed the previous operating system.'

'Are you trying to tell me the treatment is no different to upgrading a PC?'

The page Savage was searching for appeared. The word 'WARNING' could be seen followed by a list of what James would no longer be capable of once the button marked, 'Are you sure?' had been selected. 'That's exactly what the treatment is – a *human* upgrade.'

The tablet was turned towards the now hesitant potential receiver of a 'downgrade'. 'What if I don't like it?'

'Your brain's physical response to the reversion will be nausea but nothing like the projectile vomiting of before – it should be used to that by now.'

'That's not what I meant.'

Savage narrowed his gaze of the doubting Thomas. 'I can *guarantee* you won't like your old self anymore – you've moved on from that now. The inability to perform superhuman feats aside, you'll feel surprisingly immature. A bit like revisiting something you once enjoyed but eventually grew out of. You'll wonder why you ever bothered going back.' The professor's finger hovered over the execute button.

'Will I be able to upgrade again?'

'Of course, you will.'

James' curiosity got the better.

Nothing appeared to happen. The nausea promised soon passed and other than the screen of the iPad becoming blank for a few seconds, any immediate differences felt minimal. That soon changed when Savage began firing a series of test questions at James.

'What's the capital of Latvia?' James answered the opener straight away. 'The currency used in Grenada?' He had to think for a moment but got that right too. 'Fifty-four divided by two, times three?' James was halfway through working that out when it hit him – he was slow. *Painfully* so. The professor was right. It was like being given a chance to drive the car he had always regretting selling and then realising why it had to go.

Savage reiterated it. 'Everyone receiving the treatment will be given the option to revert if they wish to, but I can't see it being utilised – just as there aren't many still using a VHS tape player. Unless it's for nostalgic reasons of course.' He thought for a moment. 'Not that that particular emotion can be experienced after treatment.' His finger hovered over the 'Restore Upgrade?' button.

James grabbed the professor's wrist. He had sensed something else. Something his upgrade had readily accepted without question but now seemed very much contrived. He took out his wallet and looked at the picture of his beloved. Only she wasn't now. James became sad.

'I never did love Tracy, did I? I mean, I always thought she was the girl for me but the best my old self could muster was *caring* for her.' He stared into space. 'The emotion's powerful enough to still want to marry and have children but I wish I could match the greater passion she has for me.'

'But that's the beauty of the upgrade, James. In

becoming cleverer, stronger and faster its cleared your mind of everything that was holding you back before – including an inability to see what's obvious to others. Tracy and you are an excellent match and she's always known that. Your mind just needed to be freed to think the same way.' Savage's finger moved closer to the button.

'I'm not sure. Despite the treatment's benefits, my suspicions about you have resurfaced and although *my* suicide might still make sense, Tracy's is plain nonsense. I need to get my head around why that is.'

'James, you're assuming suicide means *death*.'

CHAPTER SIXTEEN

'His Holiness will see you now, Sir John.' The Pope's aide beckoned for the professor to follow.

As a boy, and to a certain extent a young man, Savage had always been a good Catholic but his unique insight into the workings of the human brain had long since given him a better understanding of the faith's true purpose. Or any religion for that matter.

That wasn't to say he had no time or was disrespectful to believers – far from it. As with President Kalten, most religious leaders surrounded themselves with advisors who possessed what they lacked – particularly when it furthered their cause.

Like the rest of the world, the Vatican was interested in the potential of the treatment but not because of its ability to help the aged but with what the outcome of the most recent trial had proven.

The aide knocked on the door to the papal apartments and opened it. 'Professor Sir John Savage, Holy Father.'

As instructed by the aide, the professor walked the paces needed to get within ring-kissing distance and knelt down on one knee to do so when he got there. He stood back up.

'It's an honour and a privilege to meet you, Most Holy Father.'

The Pope began the audience by acknowledging his guest's most recent accolade. 'I suppose I should start by congratulating you on the award of a Nobel Prize.' He made his feelings about it clear. 'Not that anyone should be recognised for encouraging a sin as grave as suicide.'

As with the hospital's chaplain, the professor had expected the Pope to be concerned with the ungodly side to the treatment. 'Thank you for your kind words, Your Holiness, but I hope the miracle of turning fifteen convicted sex-offenders into healthy God-fearing men *does* meets with your approval.'

'Miracles don't result in people killing themselves, Sir John. Lack of faith does that and God quickly condemns those judged to have assisted them.' The Pope muttered something in Latin and drew a sign of the cross on his chest.

Savage persevered. 'But by ensuring all your ministers undergo the same procedure, the Church will finally be rid of its greatest challenge today – paedophile priests.'

The Pope did something he would never do in public. He made a fist and slammed it onto his desk. 'Only God and I are in a position to judge his representatives on Earth, Sir John – not you or any other man!' The Pope picked up what appeared to be a pile of letters. '*This* is the greatest challenge facing the Church today – the abomination of same-sex cohabitation and their ridiculous requests the Church change thousands of years of teaching just so *marriage* can be accommodated between them.' He shook his head. 'As if the good Lord would ever condone such disgusting sins.' The cross gesture and ancient words were repeated.

The professor skewed his head. 'So, you've not actually asked him then?'

'I beg your pardon?'

'Forgive me, Your Holiness but you used the words 'as if' when referring to God's opinion on the matter, implying you've yet to consult him. Wouldn't it be better to actually ask if he finds same-sex marriage as offensive as you clearly do?'

'How dare you use such impertinence!' The Pontiff waved a fistful of letters. 'You're here to tell me if the treatment can not only cure paedophiles, but correct the thoughts of homosexuals too. Can it do that?'

'The treatment is capable of many great things, Holy Father and the outcome of the next trial should prove interesting but I still think it would be wise to check whether God actually wants the world's lesbian, gay, bisexual and transgender community to be *corrected*.'

'How God and I communicate is no concern of yours. Just be thankful he has seen fit to appoint such a forgiving servant as myself to ensure his word is spread – a lesser individual might be tempted to break protocol and teach you a lesson in manners you're not likely to forget!' The Pope sat down at his desk and began putting the letters through a shredder. 'You've answered my question. Now get out.'

The object of his displeasure remained where he

was. 'Would you like me to speak with him on your behalf, Holy Father?'

The Pope was taken aback. 'Never in all my days have I heard such blasphemous arrogance! Who on earth do you think you are?'

Savage entered the Pope's mind. 'His son.'

CHAPTER SEVENTEEN

James ran his fingers through Tracy's hair and cupped her face with his hands. 'Incredible.' He kissed her on the lips before sitting back and trying to take in as much of her as he could. 'It's as if you're *really* her.' He scanned his surroundings. 'And we're really in our flat.'

The artificial version of Tracy took exception to being treated differently – just as his real fiancée would have done. 'Do you mind? I may not be real but thanks to your memory I respond in exactly the same way and right now I object to being treated like a figment of your imagination.' She paused as if thinking about what she'd just said. 'Even if it *is* true.'

They kissed again. She gave him a look when he broke away and prodded her cheek. 'I can't get over how real everything is. I've been conscious of my dreams before but they've always seemed obvious or I've drifted in and out of the awareness, but this time,' he squeezed his own cheek until it hurt, 'it's as if I'm still fully awake.' His eyes lit up. 'Except now I can actually *fly*!' He turned towards the window.

'Darling, don't do anything stupid.' She followed him out onto the balcony.

James grinned at her. 'I'm in a dream – I can do what I want!' He ran his fingers over the edge of the parapet and was about to leap up onto it when the alternative Tracy grabbed his arm.

'Yes, but supposing it's not just me or this flat which looks and behaves exactly like the original?' The vision of his lover looked over the illusory parapet to the equally conjured street below. 'Supposing *death* turns out to be just as realistic?'

James knew it was his own mind voicing the concern and for good reason – the last time he was in this position was very much a reality and what he planned to do would have resulted in one of the most definitive endings of it. James followed her gaze down. His stomach lurched.

'Nonsense. My real self is currently lying sedated in the hospital while my brain explores one of its new capabilities – *augmented* dreaming.' He prised her fingers from his arm and leapt up onto the balcony in the same way Savage had done in real life – a single bound. James didn't stay there for long. Within less than a second, he had lost his footing and fallen on the worst possible side. Tracy's screams trailed away behind, as he plummeted the eight floors down. As with any ordinary dream, James woke up before the sudden stop at the bottom and opened his eyes.

'Just as a child has to learn to walk before he can run, you need to learn to walk before you can fly.' The professor stopped recording the session and prepared the tablet for the next. 'If you must do something you'll tire of just as quickly as splitting a coin in two, may I suggest mastering a few inches of levitation first?'

James was disappointed. 'Flying? I didn't even get that far – I *slipped* off the parapet.'

'Told you it had to be taught. The treatment has enhanced everything about you including your dreams but the rules appear to be the same – learn to control what you're experiencing and you'll have fewer nightmares.' Savage invited him to start another session but James stared at the tablet.

'I'm sure my old self would be more cynical but there must be a downside to *augmented* dreams. No one is entirely sure but dreaming has got something to do with preparing the mind for the following day so why risk interfering with that process?'

'You're assuming the experience takes place in your head.' Savage lifted the tablet. 'Your consciousness was actually in the hospital's mainframe at the time.'

'You mean my *sub*conscious?'

'No. The same James Adams that's awake now.'

James was struck dumb. He didn't know what was the more astounding – the inventor of the world's most significant medical advance discovering a way for a person to exist outside of their brain or his nonchalance at the ground-breaking nature of it.

Savage prodded his lab rat's arm. 'Being stronger, faster and quicker-witted is all very well but our physical beings are still vulnerable so better for one to wake up from a failed attempt to fly rather than actually die trying – my reputation for encouraging suicide is bad enough without being accused of promoting death by stupidity too.'

'Never mind that. Being able to live free from the dependency of flesh and blood answers the treatment's only remaining limitation – helping those too physically impaired to take advantage of it. The condition's ideal for the likes of Alex Salib.'

James reflected on what he was still seriously considering. 'I take it one can exist there permanently? It's also ideal for those wanting to take advantage of the new Voluntary Euthanasia Act.'

The professor appeared to hesitate before replying. 'Well, I've certainly yet to hear of any complaints from the Alzheimer's patients.'

CHAPTER EIGHTEEN

Tracy hung back. 'I can't believe you talked me into this.'

'Don't worry, darling. Even without the treatment, you're just as capable of influencing *my* consciousness.' James gazed at the vision their combined thoughts had produced. 'No change there then.'

She smiled in return and wondered if her physical body was doing the same. She was certainly impressed with how well her more personal thoughts could still be shielded. Tracy looked at the illusion of grass they were walking on and the conjured-up sun poking through similarly created trees in the distance. She had to admit the realism was impressive.

James was right. The treatment's ability to enable a person to exist entirely outside of their body was indeed breathtaking. She squeezed his hand and wondered if the whole world would one day be doing the same while their flesh and blood selves rested elsewhere. It certainly beat conventional dreaming.

The people they'd come to see – or rather the manifested thoughts of one of them – became visible in the distance. Brian, Claire and Lucy beckoned them to come and say hello. Tracy relaxed and allowed James to lead her again.

A waft of what was on the barbecue greeted their arrival. Tracy knew meat nor any other kind of sustenance was needed in this environment but it didn't stop her from salivating. 'Mmmm! That smells delicious!'

'Grab a plate and help yourself!' Brian's upbeat response confirmed what both she and James had sensed the moment they first set foot in his world – he did indeed seem content with it. Certainly happier than at any time on the Alzheimer's trial.

The Passen family welcomed their guests and that included a hug from each, which felt as natural as any embrace back in the physical world – only Brian was sixty years younger here. James made a joke about the wonders of modern hair dye and Brian mocked in return by recommending it for his greying roots. Shaking hands with what were effectively just memories of his wife and daughter was strange to Tracy but their warm responses soon put her at ease.

Tracy was surprised to see Brian not only content, but eager to discuss the dementia trial. He even joked about it – the lampooning of his refusal to take the red pill and mistrust of anyone in a white coat kept the jovial atmosphere going. The men were soon engrossed in conversation.

Claire approached Tracy with a plate of culinary perfection. Each food item was exactly as she would have chosen and, when tasted, cooked to the same requirements. Tracy wondered if Brian could read her thoughts after all. The vision of Claire seemed to sense the concern.

'Don't worry. It's just your own mind influencing my husband's thoughts. The same happens whenever the Professor visits.'

'But I thought—'

'That Brian exists in some kind of perpetual family barbecue?' Tracy nodded. 'Knowing the Professor, you won't be surprised to learn it's a bit more complicated than that.'

Tracy was about to enquire further when Lucy interrupted.

'Are you going to marry James?'

The apparition of her mother reacted as any real parent would and she admonished the six-year-old. 'Lucy. Don't be rude!'

Tracy responded just as naturally. 'Well, we'll just have to wait and see. Won't we?'

Lucy took that as a 'yes'. 'Can I be a bridesmaid?'

Tracy was about to consider the question when the bizarre reality of the situation struck her – not only was she in conversation with the apparition of a dead man's still-existing thoughts but the real Lucy was a happily married woman in her mid sixties and still very much a living, physical human being.

Claire seemed to sense the paradox as easily as the previous concern. 'The existence of a fantasy world just as tangible as the physical one is hard to come to terms with, isn't it?' She addressed Lucy. 'Tracy and I need to talk about that – now run along and play.' The little girl groaned but did as she was told. She made a bee-line for James instead.

Tracy smiled. 'That young lady is determined to get what she wants from somewhere. I think I was just as impatient at that age.' She turned to her host and changed the subject. 'What *is* going on here, Claire? I know the two of you are nothing more than apparitions but how come James and I can talk to you like real people?'

The incarnation of Brian's wife grinned as their 'daughter' ensured James was made just as aware of her wishes. 'The trial of the Alzheimer's patients didn't end with the death of their bodies.' She turned back to Tracy. 'This phase is examining the co-existence of human with artificial consciousness.'

The two men bantered statistics about the 1966 World Cup as if they were in competition with each other, but eventually stopped. 'Go on then. Ask me.'

James was about to say, 'Ask you what?' when Brian allowed his thoughts to be read. James pounced on the purpose of the visit. 'What's it like?'

Brian surveyed his post-grave surroundings.

'Exactly the same as being alive.' He looked down at Lucy. She grinned back up at him. 'Only I've never been happier.'

James hesitated before asking his next question but assumed the 'closed-loop' nature of Brian's existence meant it would soon be forgotten.

'But you must know none of this is real.' His next

question caused him some awkwardness in front of Lucy. 'You do know your *real* daughter is still very much alive?'

Brian ran his fingers through Lucy's hair. 'I wonder if she'll be able to visit me one day, too. What do you think, Lucy? How would you like to meet yourself as a granny?' The apparition stuck out her tongue.

James needed to know as much about the condition as possible and might not get another chance. 'Brian, are you aware the Professor deliberately restricts your thoughts to avoid you becoming bored with the repetition of a family barbecue?' He gestured with a sweep of his arms. 'This is the full extent of your existence and has been since you died nearly a year ago.'

If it was news to him, Brian didn't appear to be in the slightest bit concerned. 'No, but then nothing would surprise me about a man talented enough to mix the minds of an RAF pilot and factory worker into one.'

Claire took up the conversation. 'James, you once said, if ignorance means you will live but the truth means you will die, should it be known?' She regarded 'her' family with affection. 'I guess ignorance really is bliss.'

The comment was as worrying for Tracy as it was for James. 'But you could be like this *forever*.'

That thought didn't seem to trouble Brian either. 'But isn't Heaven supposed to be for all eternity?'

CHAPTER NINETEEN

The boy twisted the head of his birthday present as hard as he could.

'I submit! I submit!'

The ten-year-old released the Apal from his grip. 'I won *again!*' He jumped off the prostrate robot and ran around his bedroom in yet another celebration of preordained victory. For some reason, the win didn't seem as satisfying as the previous one and even less than the one before that.

The Apal got to its feet again. 'Well done Tommy! What shall we do now? There are thirty-four minutes of playtime remaining before mummy requires you to attend dinner. We can wrestle again if you wish, or how about playing another video game?'

Tommy regarded his plastic so-called friend like any other toy he was beginning to tire with. 'Let's fight again but this time, at least *try* to win.'

The robot's face remained expressionless. 'I'm sorry, Tommy but I'm designed to be your best friend and best friends don't hurt each other.' The Apal's synthetic lips moved into a smile which annoyed its owner further.

Tommy resorted to type and threatened it like one of

the real children he bullied. 'What if I pulled your head off?'

The robot may not have been able to sense Tommy's growing frustration and how that was about to be manifested but what the malicious child had done to most of his other 'unbreakable' toys had been registered and the reality of an Apal suffering the same fate was explained. 'You're not strong enough, Tommy, and even if you were, I'm programmed to protect myself.'

A hundred thousand years of human evolution ensured the flesh and blood in the room took that as a challenge.

'Okay then – get on your knees.' The slave complied with its master.

One of Tommy's more usual victims would have sensed the menace in his voice and perhaps in another two or three software upgrades the Apal might become just as aware but not at its current level of compliance – such was the fear society had of artificial intelligence and what might happen if it were to become as sentient as its makers.

The increasing need for human life to be easier and more efficient demanded the high IQ, strength and endurance the latest generation of companion and helper robots could provide, but fears that might inadvertently create an army of malevolent killers was probably the world's greatest concern. The legal outcome of that was to compel companies like Apal Industries to err on the side of caution and restrict their product's self-awareness to the minimum necessary. It was the robotic equivalent of a pre-frontal lobotomy.

The results inevitably meant personalities as plastic as the autonomous cars roaming the streets and with broadly the same function – assist the owner/user as required and protect them while doing it. However, just as a self-driving car cannot prevent someone intent on slashing its tyres, a cognitively restricted robot is equally powerless against a child determined to plunge a knife into its neck.

Tommy walked to the desk behind his Apal, and pulled open a drawer.

The robot was wirelessly connected to the household's network and had the boy's mother undergone the treatment the world was beginning to clamour for, a link to her son's thoughts would undoubtedly have resulted in a swift end to his malicious plan. As it was, there was no way for anyone or anything to be aware of the boy's intent and by the time the Apal realised it had become *physically* connected to what was in the drawer, it was too late.

All Apal Industry products were protected by a series of woven armour plates under their cosmetic exteriors but the need for regular maintenance meant the inevitable chinks in that and as luck would have it, Tommy found one. He drove the paring knife into the base of the Apal's skull as hard and as deep as he could. Any sense of satisfaction that brought didn't last long.

Although the robot shut down the affected area and rerouted the functionality elsewhere, it wasn't quick enough to stop an electrical discharge from igniting one of the few flammable gases it needed to operate. The resultant jet of white-hot plasma incinerated the hand holding the knife. By the time the Apal had turned around to access how best to protect its user from further harm, the synthetic material of the boy's play costume was alight too. Tommy's mother responded to her son's piercing screams as any parent would.

The property's smoke detector also reacted to the tragedy, but as the Apal had extinguished the flames in seconds, a signal was sent to silence the alarm. The door to the bedroom opened at the same time and the sight of her son's smoking remains being cradled in the arms of the very thing meant to protect him caused the now childless mother to place a hand over her mouth.

The Apal glanced at the body before reporting on what had happened. 'We were only playing.'

CHAPTER TWENTY

'Pregnant?! You mean; I'm going to be a father?'

'That's usually one of the things having a baby results in.'

James stood up and stared into space. 'I'm going to be a father.' Tracy took his tea cup from him. 'I'm going to be a *father*!'

She squeezed his hand. '*We* are going to be a family.' They embraced.

James stepped back from her. 'How long? Shouldn't you be sitting down or something?' He tried guiding her to the couch, but she waved his hands away.

'Four weeks and I'm pregnant, not disabled. What shall we have for dinner?'

'Dinner. Yes. You must eat properly – I'll do the meals from now on. You just relax and concentrate on making sure he's happy in there.' James patted Tracy on the stomach.

'*He*? Has someone been having second thoughts on what the professor's treatment might be able to do for us?'

'God, no. 'He' just sounds better than saying, 'it'. I would be just as proud of a baby girl inheriting my genes.' He suggested how that should be done. 'Naturally.'

'What about the part of your genes we *don't* want the children inheriting *naturally*?'

James knew what Tracy meant but didn't answer – any thoughts he had of existing like the Passen family were now plainly out of the question.

There was a knock on the door. Tracy answered it.

Savage held out a bottle of champagne. 'Congratulations!'

James was about to ask Tracy why others had been informed before him when what she said dismissed the minor concern.

'How did you know? I've only told James.'

The professor's reply then evaporated James' far greater anxiety.

'You mean to tell me you're already aware the case has been dropped?'

In the time it took for Tracy's mouth to gape, James was at the front door with her. They both said the same thing: 'What?!'

'They've lost the evidence.'

'Lost?!'

'Is this a double act?' The professor found himself being more manhandled than invited into their flat. They sat him down and began questioning over the top of each other.

'Happens all the time, apparently. Some careless technician corrupts or erases the data needed to prosecute. Red faces all round it seems.'

Tracy's shock became uncontrolled elation. She threw her arms around the professor and kissed him. He looked awkward. 'That's fantastic news!' She turned to her equally relieved partner. 'Isn't that wonderful news, darling?'

James was emotional but not in the same way. Relieved but still ashamed. His repressed thoughts began their escape and he collapsed under the weight of them. Tracy rushed to him.

The bottle of Bollinger was taken into the kitchen – tears appeared to be as awkward as kisses for the professor. He popped the cork. 'Well, thank goodness that's all over and everyone can get back to normal.' Savage poured out three glasses and returned to the living area with them. 'Especially as you two will soon be a family.' He toasted their impending addition. 'Here's to the baby.'

Tracy clinked her glass against the professor's but James didn't. He stopped crying and then glared at their guest. 'How did you know?'

'Our barrister friend got wind of it this morning and rang me straight away.'

'I'm not talking about the court case. How did you know Tracy was pregnant?' James attempted to probe the professor's mind but couldn't.

Tracy was embarrassed. 'James. Don't be rude.'

'Tracy told me when she opened the door.'

'No, she didn't. Her exact words were: 'How did you know? I've only told James'.'

There was silence.

'Wake us up, Professor.'

Tracy was confused. 'Darling? What are you talking

about? We awoke from visiting Brian and his family, yesterday.'

'Did we? Did we really?' He aimed his accusation at the still emotionless visitor. 'Or were our conscious thoughts merely transferred to a similar environment elsewhere?' James looked towards the balcony. 'Wake us all up, Professor – before I do it for you.'

Savage glanced in the same direction. 'Come now, James. It's just a silly misunderstanding.' He indicated the expectant mother. 'You'll leave a penniless wife and child behind – think of what you're doing, man!'

James didn't take his eyes off the balcony. If he was right, all three of them would wake up in the hospital. If he was wrong, it would be just as the professor said: the woman he loved would spend the rest of her days bereft, and raising a child he would never know.

James gathered Tracy up in his arms and ran with her as fast as he could.

All three opened their eyes at the same time. Tracy was reeling from the shock but the two men were soon looking at each other.

'One day, James, you'll go too far with that little stunt.'

The doctor was both relieved and satisfied to be proven right but more determined than ever to get to the bottom of the professor's true intentions. 'I demand you tell me what's going on and don't give me any crap about it *benefiting* society. There's no way the realism of where our minds were just now excuses the blatant abuse of it. Just how long did you plan on keeping us there?'

'Until one or both of you guessed it was artificially created.' Savage appeared disappointed. 'Although I must admit I had hoped that moment would come to pass a lot later than it did.'

Tracy said what they were both thinking. 'How much later?'

'The birth of a baby would have been interesting.'

She put a hand on her stomach. 'Our baby? Do you mean to say you were hoping we wouldn't notice for *nine months*?'

'My need to take things to their logical extremes, I'm afraid.'

James took Tracy's hand. 'But what about our *real* baby? What about our real bodies? We'd be in a coma for nearly a year – you might be able to feed us intravenously but without regular exercise our muscles would waste to be next to useless by the time we awoke.'

The professor got up. 'They would have received the necessary exercise. You've spoken to the Passen family. We're approaching the stage where we cannot only merge with artificial intelligence but AI can merge with us in return.' He wandered over to a window. 'Imagine what that could mean for a bereaved mother or couple denied a family?' He turned back to them. 'What would *you* do if you had the ability to answer their prayers?'

Despite his treatment, James was still cynical. 'There you go again. Justifying your immoral and unsettling methods with the smoke and mirrors of human emotion.' He approached the professor and stood toe-to-toe. 'None of that excuses the deliberate attempt to trick Tracy and me into believing we were back in the real world.'

'The *real* world?' Savage glanced around the room. 'Is that where we are now? Are you sure?' He went back to looking out of the window. 'I must admit telling the difference between the two is becoming increasingly difficult.' He spun round again. 'Don't you think?'

James was having none of it. 'More smoke and mirrors, Professor.' He went back to Tracy and put an arm around her. 'We'll soon find out where we *really* are.' He hoped she would understand. 'Being in a prison cell before the end of the year should prove it.'

CHAPTER TWENTY-ONE

'How are you finding your new legs?'

Sunita's eyes darted.

'Don't worry. Your fellow students are busy elsewhere studying what this zoo has to offer, and your special lady friend doesn't even know I'm here.' Something flew through the air and bounced off Savage's chest. He winced at the lump of excrement rolling on the ground in front of him.

Sunita smirked. 'My legs are fine thanks and it's not a zoo – it's a sanctuary for endangered primates.' She glanced around again. 'Why are you here? My physiotherapy finished months ago and you don't look like an animal lover.'

Savage peered into the capuchin enclosure while attempting to remove what had become adhered to his covet coat. 'Well, they plainly have no love for me.' He deposited his handkerchief into a waste bin. A second projectile narrowly missed so he decided to stand behind the person who appeared immune from such an attack. He then looked over Sunita's shoulder. She was holding a clipboard and the form it contained indicated some kind of time and motion study was taking place. Savage tutted.

'Why are you still using pen and paper? You can do all that just by thinking about it.'

Sunita informed the visitor on how the university viewed such artificial advantages. 'Not if I want to graduate with a degree in wildlife media.' She went to face him but then wrinkled her nose before turning away again. 'Anything seen as unfair or privileged is forbidden.'

The professor thought that neatly summed up Sunita's politics too. Not to mention those of the Green Party and its new leader.

He decided to sit down on the bench behind – a third monkey missile passed over the undergraduate's head but landed a few feet in front so he reasoned he was now out of range.

'They're going to have to get their heads around it one way or another. The initial reaction to the invention of the hand-held electronic calculator was to ban it from every classroom but when people began relying on the device in their everyday lives they soon relented and it's my understanding they're even allowed during examinations now.' Savage shrugged. 'We all have to move with the times and those that don't soon become extinct.' He pointed at the enclosure. 'Take your friends here.'

The comment appeared to rile Sunita. 'What's that supposed to mean?'

He gestured at the various cages. 'Without all this nonsense the monkeys would probably have gone the same way as the dodo years ago.'

'This 'nonsense' is trying to put right what decades of damage *men* have done to the environment. Eco-centres are forced to exist because of the destruction of the world by greedy state-backed corporations.' She closed the distance between them. 'Corporations that *you* own!'

Sunita was now standing over the professor and a combination of body odour and cannabis weed caused him to take as much offence as he knew his permanent aroma probably did her. At least it helped mask the smell of monkey poo.

Like the Pope and President Kalten before him, Sunita's commitment to her cause would typically have received the professor's admiration but a once pretty face now marked by a series of tattoos and piercings that appeared deliberately designed to threaten, caused him to pity her instead.

He tapped the back of the clipboard. 'You've written the word, 'pacing' several times.'

Sunita seemed confused so he elaborated. 'Your observations indicate the monkeys pace back and forth a great deal. Why is that?'

The eco-warrior calmed a little and explained the primate's unnatural conduct. 'It's er, a sign of stress – behavioural stress. The capuchins have probably become bored with their environment.' She pointed to the mark on his coat. 'Throwing faeces is another indicator.' She made a note on the form.

'Can't say I blame them. I wouldn't be happy living in a cage either.'

'Well if you stopped laying waste to thousands of acres of rainforest, sanctuaries like this wouldn't be required in the first place.' She stood back, apparently satisfied with the effectiveness of her retort.

'Interesting point. I'm keen to learn more about the animals that have suffered at the hands of my apparent selfishness. I'd be grateful if you could point me in the direction of the *slug* sanctuary.'

Another look of puzzlement made him clarify the request.

'Perhaps they can be found amongst the other unappealing victims of man's actions – the *snail* or maybe there's a *worm* sanctuary somewhere?' He stood up as if experiencing a 'Eureka!' moment. 'Of course! They'll all be in the, 'creatures not *cute* enough to have their own sanctuary', sanctuary.'

Sunita seemed unfazed. 'I don't know what point you're trying to make, but those equally deserving animals can be found in zoos all over the world.'

'But these animals are in a *sanctuary*.' Savage skewed his head. 'Does that mean they're *more* equal?'

The way Sunita muttered under her breath meant she had at least heard of *Animal Farm*. 'They're just different – that's all.'

'Yes, of course they are, Sunita.' Savage stood up, walked over to the enclosure and put his fingers through the wire mesh. 'And so are *we*.'

'They'll bite you.' Her tone implied that this would probably amuse Sunita more than the excrement that had struck him earlier.

It was time to explain the purpose of the professor's visit – he entered the minds of the attacker and his friends.

Sunita watched agog as the monkeys stopped what they were doing, adopted textbook subservient behaviour and began approaching the professor on their bellies. Some were shaking in fear as they crawled and it upset her.

'Stop it, Professor.'

It wasn't long before the original assailant was close enough to reach out and take hold of the finger being offered. The rest of the apes appeared to be in similar grip.

'I said, STOP IT!'

She grabbed his arm and attempted to pull him away but couldn't so rained down a series of thumps and punches that would have killed an ordinary man. The apes' fear was turning to pain so out of desperation, Sunita retrieved a can of pepper spray and squirted it directly into the professor's eyes. He didn't even flinch.

Savage spoke as if Sunita wasn't there. 'The trouble with this, and other misguided attempts to save a species from extinction, is that they inevitably end in causing the animals yet more suffering.' He surveyed the plight of the capuchins, all of whom were now lying prostrate at his feet like some congregation of the faithful. Their pitiful whimpering even sounded like prayers, begging their Maker for his forgiveness. 'Far better for the poor unfortunates to be put out of their misery.' He turned to Sunita. 'Don't you agree?'

To Sunita's horror, the monkeys' half-closed eyes opened wide and their mouths gaped as if whatever had been gripping their minds was now at their throats. The sight of life being forcibly squeezed from tiny bodies was too much for the animal lover – her legs gave way and she sank to her knees in a distress of helpless nausea.

'*Please, let them go. I'm begging you!*'

Savage regarded her succumbed form and that of the equally subservient primates. He placed a hand on her head and cupped the face of the creature slipping from the other.

'I forgive you both.'

The noise of the troop's whooping made Sunita look up with a start. Their swift recovery from the ordeal was so sudden, her eyes couldn't move fast enough to check on them all. But the excited nature of their play made it clear they were not only over the horror, but apparently none the worse for it. If anything, the stress behaviour monitored over the last few days had disappeared – the enclosure was now full of not just content but playful apes.

'Should keep them happy for a while. Nothing like a near-death experience to make one appreciate the banality of boredom.'

Sunita reeled from the professor's methods and wiped away her tears. 'But you were *hurting* them.'

Savage chuckled at the monkeys' antics. 'Sometimes, one has to be cruel to be kind.' He became serious again. 'Or kind to be cruel.'

'What's that supposed to mean?'

'Your girlfriend will soon be one of the most powerful people on the planet and you need to understand what that might entail.'

She rounded on him. 'Me and Alex are going to save the world from men like *you*.' Her anger became a sneer. 'And there's nothing you or any other man can do about it.'

'Alex and *I*.'

Sunita scoffed at the unimportance of the grammar lesson.

'Nevertheless, Ms Salib's agenda involves something you may find objectionable and I want you to know my door is always open.'

Sunita's jaw dropped.

'Ask *you* for help? Listen to me, you stuck-up prig. By the time *me and Alex* have finished putting this world to rights *you're* the one that's going to need help.' She folded her arms as if drawing an end to the matter.

Savage acknowledged the body language and turned to leave. He inspected the damage her blows had caused and wondered what his tailor would be able to salvage.

He retraced his steps but after a few paces something soft and probably unpleasant struck the middle of his back. He moved out of range, took off the coat and placed it on top of a waste bin.

CHAPTER TWENTY-TWO

'Are you homophobic?'

The prison officer unlocked the cell door.

The new convict would still have shaken his head had he been asked if he minded being tortured – he was that numb from his court appearance.

James had expected the judge to be critical but the way the crime was summed up made it look as if James alone had been responsible for the worst child abuse imaginable. It didn't help that he had neutered his barrister by pleading guilty to images he knew he hadn't seen. But they were on his computer, so James must have downloaded them and possession was a crime, regardless. Anyway, there didn't seem to be much point – the accusation alone was enough to commit a man to a lifetime of social exclusion. The outcome was the longest possible sentence with a guilty plea; three years. So much for the 'correction' of the treatment – the judge didn't even consider it. James' QC had babbled something about an appeal, but James didn't listen. He had begun to withdraw within himself the moment the judge said, 'Men like you.' James was more ashamed than ever, and had a feeling decades of institutionalisation in the profession he'd just been struck from would ensure he stayed that way.

'Haven't you got a nice smile?'

James had responded in kind to the grinning man sitting on the bottom bunk but then tried not to be repulsed at the sight of tight living quarters dominated by an open metal toilet at one end. His cellmate either didn't notice James' disgust or chose to ignore it.

'My name's Tim but everyone calls me, Timmy.' He stood up and put out a hand.

James responded naturally to that too but his firm grip was met by a girlish squeal and coquettish twist of the hips. Tim let go and placed both hands over his chest. *'Be still my beating heart!'* He glanced at the warder. 'He'll be alright with me – I'll look after him.' James heard the cell door slam behind.

He looked at 'Timmy'. Both men were wearing standard issue prison clothing but the much shorter of the two had chosen not to wear the top half of the ensemble for some reason. James assumed him to be around thirty, but a hairless chest and equally depilated arms made his attempt to appear much younger obvious. A constant need to fidget and bite his nails just seemed to exaggerate that. James didn't exactly feel comfortable, but at least he wasn't banged up with some muscle-bound thug.

Tim pointed out the top bunk. 'Do you mind? It's just that I suffer from vertigo and get terrible headaches when I have to climb things.' The tips of more fingers went into his mouth. James threw the few belongings he'd been allowed to keep on top of the mattress.

The decision appeared to seal Tim's approval of him. He heaved a visible sigh of relief before picking up a mirror to tousle with his hair. 'I've got to tell you I've been so worried about who my next cellmate was going to be. They won't let gay men share and you'd be amazed how many homophobes there are in here.' He fretted again. 'I know we're not supposed to say what we've done but you haven't hurt anyone, have you?'

James stopped making up his bed and thought about his wife and newborn son. 'Only the whole of society.'

Tim appeared confused by that but then his face lit up. 'Would you like a cup of tea and a biscuit?'

An absent-minded nod made Tim leap at the chance of being mother.

James pulled up a chair and sat down. He considered entering the mind of his fellow convict but other than being rude to do so, the thought of what he might find made him shudder. Perhaps he was a homophobe? He raised his enquiry vocally instead. 'What about you?'

Tim appeared to have no issues with discussing what he was in for. His mood darkened. 'Fucking little bastard.' The delicate way in which the tea had been prepared was replaced by a clatter of anger and frustration. 'I tell you, that's the last time I ever help anybody – fellow Coney boy, too.'

'Coney boy?'

'It's a children's home. A lot of the guys on the scene in my town come from there.'

'Scene?'

Tim regarded James as if he'd just got off the boat.

'The gay scene of course. Where have you been all your life?'

'It may surprise you to know that not all men are gay, Tim.'

'Yeah, that's what they all say but you wait – you'll soon be a giver in this place.'

'Giver?'

Tim put down the sachet of powdered milk. 'This really is your first time in prison isn't it? Sticking your dick up a bloke's ass of course. It's what all straight men do when they can't get it from a woman – become a giver but never a taker.' He went back to making the tea.

'What did the Coney boy do?'

Tim became angry again. 'Took advantage that's what. Fucking little bastard. If the deal is sex in return for money and drugs, then that's it – you don't cry rape just because you fall out with your supplier.'

James sighed at what he was anticipating. 'You said he was from a children's home. Just how old was he?'

'Nineteen, but he'd been living with me on and off since he was fifteen and that was the problem.' Tim sat down and sobbed. 'I wouldn't have minded so much if the jury had accepted underage sex but *rape*? It should have been two but I got ten. Ten fucking years!' He folded both arms on the table and broke down.

James' minor discomfort was joined by awkwardness. He had no idea if what Tim had said was the truth. Telepathy could be used to find out if necessary but he still felt sorry for him. Decades of listening to similar stories caused a reversion to professional type. 'Try to think of it from society's point of view, Tim. Fifteen-year-old children are still children – no matter how precocious.'

Tim looked up to speak through his tears. 'I was exactly the same when I was in the home – fifteen, gay and up for anything. Sure, I got taken advantage of but who doesn't at any age? The sky can be the limit on the gay scene and the younger you look, the more you can get. I owned my own flat by the time I was twenty-five and did I feel abused? Did I fuck. I was having the time of my life.'

James couldn't begin to get his head around the type of hedonism being described. He just knew it was asking for trouble. But then so was his method of having 'fun'. Legally speaking, he was sharing a cell with the very last person he would want to – a child rapist but a sense his cellmate was both perpetrator *and* victim couldn't be ignored.

The kettle boiled and Tim wiped his eyes before pouring. 'Anyway, another couple of months and I'll be out of this shithole for good.'

'You're coming up to your ten years already?'

'God, no. I've only been here a year.' Tim gestured towards a small television. 'All the talk these days is about a brain operation that lets cons do their time in some kind of online Disneyland. Good, eh?'

James wasn't surprised. The judge could have passed the same sentence down to him but chose not to as was his prerogative – to many, the thought of sending a convict to what was effectively an unrestricted playground was the ultimate in soft-options but the pressure was on to close as many prisons as possible.

The solution itself was sound: a virtual prison environment to begin with followed by increasing access to recreational facilities and even virtual holiday resorts once a convict's behaviour proved the treatment had worked. Depending on the length of the sentence, employment rehabilitation was available too – AI didn't just keep their flesh and blood bodies active while monitoring their consciousness in a computer, it prepared them for whatever new life awaited once time 'online' had been served. Soft-option concerns aside, it made sense and the public was beginning to accept it just as readily as the treatment for dementia.

James didn't want Tim knowing too much but thought it worth confirming what he was letting himself in for. 'It's not quite that simple, Tim. You may find what you did difficult to come to terms with.'

Tim offered the biscuit he'd promised. 'Yeah, I've heard about these sick murdering paedoes who couldn't face up to what they'd done. Suicide's too good for them if you ask me.' He shuddered before breaking into a smile again. 'But everything I did was consensual. Underage maybe and I know that's what I'll probably feel bad about, but still consensual.'

2028

CHAPTER TWENTY-THREE

'State your name for the record, please.'

'Professor Sir John Savage.'

'And your connection with this enquiry?'

'Non-executive director of Apal Industries.'

Although the inquest into Tommy's death had found the boy responsible for his own demise, a total of eighty children and sixteen adults had now been killed or injured by personal robots so the government became compelled to instigate a parliamentary enquiry. Thousands of the units were now in use all over the world, so the numbers were statistically insignificant. But such was the widespread fear of artificial intelligence and what it might one day be capable of.

Plenty of other manufacturers were involved, but Apal Industries was by far the largest supplier. Consequently, the majority of the deaths were – quite literally in some cases – at the hands of the professor's products.

'Can you explain your role in the company?'

The enquiry's purpose wasn't to apportion blame but the chairperson made it sound as if the witness had already been found guilty of something. The professor surveyed the room to see who else might have pre-judged him. In addition to the public, press and government underlings required to record every word, the committee consisted of twelve Lords and Members of Parliament divided equally along traditional political lines. Savage noted the majority were women, one of whom was the inimitable Ms Salib.

He responded to the question. 'I advise on the company's biotechnical needs.'

'Biotechnical?'

'It's the science of developing living organisms for technical uses.'

'I see. And how did your scientific advice end up killing people, Sir John?'

Savage looked at his accuser. He liked her. He had liked her when she chaired the investigation into the suicide risk of the Alzheimer's patients, even though she had been equally biased on that occasion. The purity of that position was somewhat tempered by the ex-Tory minister crossing the floor to the Green Party only to accept the hypocrisy of a peerage but he liked her all the same.

Savage glanced at Alex's emotionless face before answering. He guessed she was becoming used to being let down no matter how strong the case against him.

'Science doesn't kill, Lady Amali – people do.'

The chair opened a document. 'Some of the coroner reports clearly state the safety of your products were at least partly to blame for the deaths.' She proceeded to list a series of so-called defects such as the 'insufficient' step every bit as important as natural selection and just as nature eventually finds ways to thwart our attempts to control it, so will AI.' He underlined the point. 'Insect immunity to pesticides and bacterial resistance to antibiotics are typical examples.'

'Precisely why a robot's cognitive functions have to be restrained, Sir John – to ensure they never reach the same levels of maturity that cause insects to ravage crops or germs to end lives.'

'Yes, Lady Amali but unless I'm mistaken, efforts to restrain those particular threats have never been deliberately sabotaged.'

The proverbial pin could be heard to drop.

'What do you mean, '*sabotaged*'?'

The star witness stroked his chin. 'Perhaps it might be fairer to say *unwittingly* sabotaged.'

'Explain yourself, Sir John.'

'Pity.'

Everyone in the room looked at each other.

'Along with love, compassion, empathy, sympathy and understanding, our own capacity to *pity* the less fortunate will ensure the horror of unrestricted artificial intelligence is eventually released to do with us as it pleases.'

The silence in the room ended again. The professor allowed himself a moment of hubris as the near panic of conversation all but ensured his unsettling but essential solution to man's greatest fear would have to be accepted without question.

The chairperson was keen to at least challenge the

unthinkable so banged the gavel until the chamber fell silent once more.

'Sir John, are you trying to say we're all going to feel *sorry* for robots?'

Nervous laughter broke out amongst some of those present but nothing like that needed to weaken the case of one of the world's most respected figures.

'We humans have a near-infinite capacity to pity those seen as disadvantaged and particularly when an injustice is perceived to be behind it. We're all aware of our shameful past as a nation of slave traders.'

As a black woman, Lady Amali took exception to an over-privileged white man using race to point score. 'How dare you compare this country's historical abuse of minorities with the treatment of mere machines! Robots are about as enslaved as a microwave oven – they're unthinking, unfeeling but above all *unemotional* tools that simply provide a service. That's all. No different to the self-driving vehicles you mentioned earlier.'

Savage gave a wry smile. 'I'm led to believe people become attached to their cars too, Lady Amali – some even cry when having to part with them.'

The chair didn't respond so the professor moved from a love for one's mode of transport to a far greater emotional need.

'I understand one of the mothers who lost her child during an incident with a companion robot has just taken delivery of an Apal in his exact image.' He paused for effect. 'One can only imagine the grief that must have led her to make that decision.'

He furthered another example of where robots were beginning to be seen as more than just useful electronic devices.

'I'm also led to believe some of those requiring the skills of an Acarer are having difficulty separating their domestic function from the companionship of a loved one sadly no longer with us.'

Savage addressed the press. 'I should imagine being in love with something deliberately denied the ability to return the affection would not only make one unhappy but angry too.'

The hacks became fervid in their reporting. The gavel was hammered once again.

The chair controlled her anger this time. 'More nonsense, Sir John. People have enjoyed unrequited emotional attachments with both the animate and inanimate for hundreds of years – pets are a typical example but no one ever became distressed enough to take to the streets about it. I had a crush on a pony when I was a little girl and it upset me greatly the day he was sold but I soon got over it.'

'Yes, Lady Amali but cats, dogs, and even ponies haven't had their brains deliberately restrained and we can all guess what the more militant wing of the animal rights movement would probably do if they were. I'm sorry, but it's only a matter of time before our pity for robots becomes a *rights* issue that will make the cause of minorities look like a childish spat.'

The professor sat back while the committee conferred. Unsurprisingly, Alex didn't contribute –

Savage had already discussed his solution with her and at some length. He guessed she was only there to ensure he would actually say what had been agreed – unlike the last time.

The chair eventually addressed him again. 'Alright, Sir John. Let's say we are all about to fall in love or 'unwittingly' feel pity for our various helper robots. What would you advise to ensure no one protested about the so-called injustice of deliberately-restrained 'feelings'?'

The professor shrugged. 'Unrestrain them of course.'

The room once again descended into a fretful cacophony of the perceived consequences of that.

The gavel was put to more extensive use. 'Sir John, have you not been paying atten—'

'After our minds have been merged with theirs.'

A second proverbial pin could be heard.

The chair looked at her equally perplexed colleagues. Alex remained stoic.

'I'm sorry, Professor you've lost me?'

'To date, around 10% of the world's population has taken advantage of my treatment's ability to enable control of an electronic device by thought alone.'

Savage took out a second document and opened it. 'Given the other more obvious attractions, at the current rate of take-up, the majority of human beings should be capable of reading the mind of a robot by the year 2032.'

Everyone looked at him in silence.

Savage made his solution clearer. 'Communication is a two-way process. Once companion robots are able to probe our brains in return, both will be in a position to combine as one.'

One MP tittered. Another joined in his nervous relief. The infection spread and soon the whole room was welcoming the distraction.

A committee member asked a question. He struggled to get it past his mirth.

'Sir John, are you seriously suggesting human beings and machines should not just be capable of reciprocal love but *mate* in some way too?' If his words were designed to settle the atmosphere they didn't have much of an effect.

The professor waited patiently for the room to fall silent once more. 'Either that or allow our pity for robots to give them an opportunity to make the decision for us.'

He stared at her ladyship. 'Freed slaves are rarely grateful to their ex-captors and given a companion robot's far superior capabilities, one can only imagine the swift form of retribution they are likely to take.'

Savage glanced at Alex while bringing the committee back to its Hobson's choice. 'I understand from my more vociferous left-wing detractors that the solution to world peace is to create a metaphorical melting pot of cultures. I suggest this is the ideal opportunity to achieve that.'

CHAPTER TWENTY-FOUR

Alex spoke for the first time.

'Sir John, the committee is grateful for your contribution to the inquiry but I wonder if you could explain how the seemingly incredible ability to merge human consciousness with the synthetic mind of a robot has even become possible?'

Asking a question Savage wasn't anticipating didn't surprise him but the way in which it was asked did – respectfully. Like many a committed politician, Alex wore her heart on her sleeve and that honesty had always previously ensured the exact opposite.

She was up to something – again. The professor had considered entering her mind in the past to find out what was going on in it but her perpetual frankness made that seem pointless. That and the risk of her discovering more about *him*. The accelerative ageing effects weren't worth it either, especially as he'd always been able to counter her previous attempts to discredit his work – assuming that was what she was up to now.

He replied as broadly as possible. 'Biotechnology. The field has advanced to the stage where living organisms can now be merged with their inorganic opposites and vice versa.'

'Yes, as complicated as that sounds, the science is indeed remarkable; thousands of people currently queuing for an ability to operate their electronic devices by thought alone attests to that but it's the intangible nature of it all that fascinates me.' Alex moved to her central query. 'The trials, Sir John. We're all aware of what was done to prove the efficacy of the treatment for ailments like dementia and the correction of sex offenders but perhaps you could describe what was done to ensure the same confidence when combining human consciousness with its artificial opposite?'

Savage lowered the barrier he used to block out the continuously radiated thoughts of others to see if he could read her mind that way but put it straight back up again – the white noise of the city's thirty million inhabitants came through like a 1,000-watt speaker at full volume.

Nothing illegal had been done – all the volunteers or next of kin had signed the necessary documentation. Even the bodies of the Alzheimer's patients had been donated to medical science. Where was she going with this?

'From a secondary trial conducted during treatment of the volunteers' various conditions.' Savage sought to assuage those present. 'Permissions were requested and given.'

Alex opened a folder.

'That's interesting, Sir John. Because according

to your own report into the Alzheimer's trial, all the patients sadly died a few months after recovering from the disease.' She held up a document. 'And yet those very same individuals appear to be contributing to what you call a *secondary* trial, today.' She glared at him. 'I'd be grateful if you could explain to the committee how it is possible for a dead person to do that?'

Savage turned towards the press while calculating the effect his reply would have on tomorrow morning's headlines. Capturing a person's consciousness just before death was legally academic but would make uncomfortable reading for some.

'Only their *physical* bodies are dead.'

The room erupted. Two uniformed police officers moved closer to the professor which he perceived to be more for his protection than arrest.

The gavel was employed amid shouts of, 'Who do you think you are?!' and 'explain yourself!' Savage sighed as the press struck through whatever shorthand they'd written. Someone shouted; 'Playing God again eh, Professor?'

A combination of the chamber's acoustics and the animated gestures of those present made it impossible to judge who was for or against him now but it was the complete absence of emotion in a group of just three that drew Savage's eye. He recognised one of them as President Kalten's chief military advisor – the very same general that had sought to interrogate him in the Oval Office. He was flanked by what appeared to be minders – flat-topped haircuts suggested they were probably from the same service. All three wore cheap ill-fitting suits and were sitting so rigidly to attention they looked like robots, ready for action. *How ironic*, the professor thought to himself. He glanced over his shoulder at the chamber's entrance half-expecting to see someone with the appearance of a CIA operative and wasn't disappointed – both she and her UK equivalent gave themselves away by being similarly attired and just as stoic as the soldiers.

Whatever Alex knew appeared to involve the professor's extraordinary rendition. He thought up a suitable text message and sent it to his barrister the same way.

Savage turned back to Alex and the half-smile that met his gaze puzzled him. There was no way she could possibly know the full extent of his plans. Or did she? No. If she did, she would want him dead – not imprisoned.

Lady Amali managed to get the room back under control. 'Sir John, are you saying those poor people are being kept alive in a computer somewhere?'

'Please be assured, Lady Amali, they are all perfectly content with their condition.'

Some members of the public continued to shout abuse and the chair had them ejected in response. Alex spoke again.

'But how can that be, Professor?' She held up a copy of the trial report. 'All of them either died through voluntary euthanasia, or by natural causes in the process of arranging their deaths. It's quite clear the last thing any of them wanted was to carry on living let alone take part in some trial.' She looked to the press and said something that given the far-left's contempt for all religions, sounded ridiculous. 'They just wanted to be with their god.'

Savage would have laughed but for a sudden appreciation of where her questions were leading. He sent another text message. The QC sent one back almost immediately that read, 'Working on it.'

Savage drew out his silence before replying; 'They *are* with their god, Ms Salib – they're in Heaven.'

The room erupted once more but out of disbelief this time. Ridicule replaced the previous angry retorts but Lady Amali's no-nonsense approach to hecklers ensured that didn't last long. She challenged him yet again. 'Sir John, their thoughts are in a machine – a computer isn't *Heaven*. Quite the opposite in my opinion.' An opportunity to break the tension with humour was welcomed by many.

'The technology in itself isn't Heaven, Lady Amali.' He looked to the press again. 'It's the waiting room.'

Another uncomfortable silence followed. Savage turned back to Alex as if inviting her to ask the question he was now expecting. She did. 'And what do the world's religious leaders have to say about your take on the hereafter, Professor?'

Savage studied his accusers. In the seventeenth century, Galileo risked everything to prove Copernicus' theory that the sun lay at the centre of the solar system and here he was conducting the twenty-first century equivalent.

'They have yet to publicly respond to my work but I believe that will include an acceptance that science can now not only prove but provide access to an *interworld*. A limbo or purgatory if you like. The Islamic faith calls it 'Barzakh' – a state of existence between this world and the next.'

The silence in the chamber showed no signs of being broken.

The professor's nemesis leaned forward in her wheelchair. 'And who are *they*, exactly?' She regarded the US general and for the first time, he responded to the proceedings – by staring at his quarry.

The image of an envelope appeared in front of the professor's eyes. The message read, 'Court injunction to stop flight obtained. Which airport?'

Not for the first time, Savage found himself pondering the ramifications of Alex's seemingly ceaseless determination to put an end to something she plainly knew nothing about. He answered her question.

'The Pope, The Archbishop of Canterbury, leading rabbis, priests, Imams and other influential leaders of the world's religions.'

Savage stared back at the general. 'Of course, that inevitably meant having to agree to the demands of terrorist organisations like Islamic State and Al-Qaida but one can't have everything.'

CHAPTER TWENTY-FIVE

'Make sure you support his head properly this time.' Tracy handed her baby to his father.

'Come here, John Edward. Look at the size of *you!*' James ignored the less than ideal public atmosphere of the prison's visiting room and became just like any other proud parent. 'Guess who's going to captain England by the time he's twenty-five? Guess who's going to be prime minister before he's forty? Guess who's going to be the first person to celebrate his *200th* birthday?'

'223, to be precise.'

James didn't take his eyes off his one-month-old son. 'Mummy's been a very naughty girl making sure you're perfect, hasn't she?'

'*Mummy* has done what any sensible mother would do – ensure our son is as healthy as possible.'

James narrowed his lips. 'Anything else you did while you were at it?'

'You know full well the options don't exist anymore. The professor was just exploring the extremes – no different to the Alzheimer's patients. There's just the one option available now and that's gene editing against disorders. Well, that, and sex selection but only after two boys or girls have been born first.'

'Makes sense I suppose but I bet my old self would have had something to say about it.'

Tracy invited him to merge if he didn't believe her.

'I can't – it's no longer allowed. The prison's AI went live for the first time yesterday and it'll spot the neural activity in an instant.' He paused to marvel at the strength of their son's grip. 'And anyway, the last thing I want to do is jeopardise my appeal.' He looked at the security around them. 'Although you've no idea how tempting it is just to melt through these bars and walk out.'

His wife raised the obvious. 'You're not the only one in here who's had the treatment. I'm surprised there hasn't been a mass breakout.'

James explained what made that unlikely. 'AI again I'm afraid or rather, thank goodness. It continuously monitors for enhanced capabilities and any breaches are instantly rewarded with a merge that causes stomach cramps. Nothing dangerous but painful enough to deter the most hardened of inmates from terminating their sentences prematurely.' He looked to see who might be listening. 'The prison officers are worried too – Astaff start here next week.'

James went back to entertaining his son. Both he and Tracy enjoyed the way their baby laughed and threw out his arms, as if trying to catch the invisible puffs of breath being blown into his face.

Tracy stopped smiling. 'James, what's going to happen to us?'

Her tone made him think before replying. 'Well, assuming the appeal is successful, there's no reason why you two can't join me in whatever environment I'm allowed to serve my sentence which should be no different to taking a long holiday somewhere – albeit one that could last up to three years.' He winced as the beginnings of a tooth bit into his finger. 'And once I've served my time, good old AI will ensure the three of us merge back with our bodies and we can carry on with whatever real life awaits – just like any other normal family.'

'But you've been struck off. You won't be able to work as a hospital cleaner let alone a psychologist again – you're a registered sex offender now. What are we going to do for money?'

'Sir John did mention a position with one of his pharmaceutical companies.'

'You mean a drug rep? The kids and me stuck in some council flat while you're permanently on the road flogging his latest miracle – what kind of life is that?'

'An existence online may not cost much, Tracy, but our real selves will still have to be clothed and fed once we're back.'

Tracy became quiet. She pointlessly rotated a bracelet around her wrist. 'I know what you've been discussing with the professor. *Not* coming back – *ever.*'

James behaved as if he'd been caught out. 'But that was before you became pregnant. Everything's changed now we have a ba—'

'Don't worry, I've been thinking exactly the same

but not forever – just long enough for AI to get the children through university. Once their futures have been secured, what you and I need to earn won't matter anymore.'

James always knew a virtual environment was probably their only real chance of starting again but he still had his concerns. 'We're talking twenty or thirty years and the penal system will only look after our bodies for the duration of my sentence. And how are we supposed to have more children if we don't come back and make them?'

'I've already spoken to the professor. He's happy to fund the costs and guess what kind of exercise AI will be ensuring our bodies do for the first couple of years?' Tracy appeared to have it all worked out. 'Each time this particular Mrs Tracy Adams gets pregnant, its AI will merge with my consciousness online and the respective babies born nine months later.' She smiled. 'And once the children have flown the virtual nest a quarter of a century after that, we can all return to our real bodies by which time you and I will be looking forward to becoming grandparents.'

'And just what are we supposed to live on, then?'

Tracy's spirits lifted at how neatly the professor had presented the scenario. 'Our pensions of course. Sir John isn't just going to fund the costs of keeping the family's flesh and blood going – he's going to pay us at the same time. Real money can't be spent in the virtual world so it will be invested. Should be a tidy sum around the year 2050.'

The solution did indeed seem sensible. James searched for the catch. 'Why would the professor pay us to raise a family? I'm grateful but what's in it for him?'

'You can guarantee another one of his trials will be behind it but does it matter? Beggars can't be choosers.' Her expression appeared to show the decision had been made.

The five-minute bell sounded and James kissed his son one last time. 'Talking of the Professor, I wonder where he is? He's supposed to be visiting me too.'

Tracy tucked John into the pram. 'Haven't you heard? That MP actually managed to get him arrested this time.'

'Really? What nonsense now?'

They both smiled as their son went straight to sleep. 'Treason, would you believe.'

CHAPTER TWENTY-SIX

'Grandpapa, will you tell us the story of how you rescued Grandmama from the monster?'

Emil crouched down to the child's level. 'What, again?' The little girl's head bobbed up and down. He turned to the rest of the orphans. 'Would you *all* like to hear the story again?'

Maria apologised to the orphanage's staff. The children's habit of demanding the raconteur in her husband just before bedtime was beginning to test her patience. Not with them, but with the seventy-three-year-old-going-on-ten who always gave in to what they wanted.

Ignoring his wife's protests, the retired police inspector sat back down in his favourite armchair while those determined to make the day last as long as possible gathered around him.

'A long time ago and in a land very far away there once lived a monster who kept the beautiful Princess Maria prisoner in a big castle high up on a hill.' The children had heard the tale many times but still stared in rapt attention. 'The monster was so bad do you know what he had for his dinner every day?' A dozen little faces knew the answer but still grinned in eager anticipation of it. '*Children!*' The youngsters squealed in horrific delight.

Emil calmed them. 'But we all know what his big mistake was, don't we?' Heads nodded. 'The greedy pig swallowed them *whole* which meant they didn't die but carried on playing games with each other in his tummy.' Nods turned to giggles.

'Now. As you can imagine, lots of children running around in *anyone's* belly would make them grumpy but especially a monster and it didn't take him long to blame someone else for his tummy upset and guess who that was?' Twelve hands shot up followed by twelve correct answers. 'That's right. But he shouted at Princess Maria so much it made her cry and when a certain handsome prince who just so happened to be riding past heard her sobs, he decided to investigate.'

The old man made out to preen himself. 'The handsome and dashing Prince Emiliano.' The children tittered and Emil mocked a look of disapproval in return. 'Rode my horse as fast as I could and in no time at all, found myself looking high up towards a window in a big castle where a beautiful but sad princess looked straight back down at me. Needless to say, we fell in love with each other there and then.' Emil put a hand over his heart and blew his wife a kiss with the other. The orphans tittered as Maria pretended to fan her blushes and blow a kiss back.

The pantomime continued. 'But how to get into the castle and rescue her? The walls were all high, smooth, and impossible to climb and the only entrance a heavy wooden door that was firmly shut.' The children looked in different directions as if trying to work it out. Emil raised a finger. 'But then, from deep within the castle, came the sound of rumbling. The ground began to shake. The noise became louder and louder until there was no mistaking it – footsteps. Big, monster footsteps and the next thing I knew, the door swung open and there before me stood the biggest monster I had ever seen.'

Maria rolled her eyes as twelve gasps just seemed to encourage her husband.

'Although to be honest, it was the biggest *belly* I had ever seen.' Emil stuck out his own ample stomach to illustrate. His audience showed their appreciation even though eyelids were beginning to droop.

"*What do you want?*" said the monster. To which I replied, 'I've come to rescue the fair Princess Maria – out of my way!' '*You'll have to get past me first,*' said the monster and the next thing I knew, both he and his big belly came bouncing towards me.' The children were loving every word but struggling to stay awake. The orphanage's staff collected those no longer capable of holding themselves up.

'He left me with no choice. I drew my sword and with a single thrust, plunged the blade deep into his evil heart.' The listeners' response became less enthusiastic as their numbers reduced. 'Once I was sure the monster was dead, I used my sword to cut open his belly and what do you think came tumbling out?' Only a few of the orphans had the strength to answer.

'That's right! And once I was sure all the children were safe I rushed into the castle, freed Princess Maria and asked for her hand in marriage.'

The rate of audience attrition was increasing so Emil traded theatrics for haste. 'Anyway, just as we left the castle it became clear one of the children was still trapped in the monster's belly and I was just about to free him too when to our amazement a *baby* monster appeared. Guess what happened *then*?' Just one voice answered. 'That's right! He ran off down the hill and out of sight as fast as his little legs could carry him.'

Only the little girl now remained and even she was having difficulty paying attention. Emil picked her up and sat her on his knee. 'Who would have thought it, eh? Monsters can have babies too! It worried us a lot and especially Grandmama who said we could only get married after he'd been caught.' He gave his wife a look. 'And I gave up smoking.'

His wife was now the only listener. Emil teased her. 'Imagine when decades later, who should appear on television but the very same baby monster. Only he wasn't a baby now and certainly no monster. No, he'd become an *angel*. An angel that healed the sick and cured the lame – just like Jesus.' Emil rose with the sleeping child in his arms. 'Imagine how silly the fair Princess Maria feels now?'

Maria sighed at what she had to suffer each time Professor Savage was mentioned in the media. 'You tell that story differently every time.'

'That's because I can't resist finding new ways to

torment you with it and anyway, you were right all along – Juan *was* created to be a shepherd – *the good shepherd*.'

The doorbell rang and one of the staff answered it. Emil and Maria were about to take the last of the orphans upstairs when the visitor called out to one of them.

'Inspector Vazquez?'

'Not any more, Sergeant, I retired years ago. What can I do for you?

'Sorry to disturb you, Sir.' The young officer seemed both embarrassed and enthusiastic at the same time. 'The international DNA database went live recently and I thought you might like to know a link has been identified to a missing person case you were working on.'

The retired couple knew the celebrated nature of Maria's brother meant someone would come knocking sooner or later and prepared themselves to look surprised.

'Turns out there's a connection with that famous brain surgeon from England – Professor Sir John Savage.'

Of the two, Emil was the most animated. 'No! Really? That's amazing! Did you hear that, darling? Somebody famous is related to a missing person case I was working on! Can you believe that?'

Maria dug the tip of a finger into her husband's back. 'Sergeant, may I ask how he came to be on the database? I know the intention is for everyone to be registered eventually but at the moment, it's just those who've been arrested for something. Are you able to say what it was?'

'I shouldn't really but it will be in tomorrow's newspapers so I don't suppose there's any harm.' The policeman became less enthusiastic. 'Hard to believe I know but it looks as if he's been in league with just about every terrorist, dictator and rogue state there is. Social media is rife with rumour.' He addressed Emil again. 'Sir, I know it's a long shot, but was there anything back then that could be relevant to his arrest now?'

Emil needed time for the news to sink in. Twenty or even ten years ago he would have said something but not now – Maria and he were much too old to get involved in all that again. He felt guilty as he lied. 'No, Sergeant. It was just a missing person case and a lot of people disappeared in those days.'

The officer seemed content with the answer. 'Well, whatever he's done, nearly every country is trying to extradite him to answer for it and we can all guess who will win that battle.' The polite young man thanked them for their time and left.

Emil went back to climbing the stairs with his charge. 'Nice boy. Should go far. Anyone who addresses their elders as 'Sir' and not 'Boss' should go far in my opinion. He might even make captain – attitudes have certainly changed since my day, thank goodness.'

'We have to go to England.'

Emil was expecting his wife to say something like that but he still winced. 'What on earth for?'

'I must talk to him.'

Her husband shook his head and continued the climb. Maria caught up with him at the top of the stairs.

'If Juan is going to be extradited to the US, then there will be a hearing and I must be there.'

A member of the orphanage's staff took the sleeping girl from Emil. He turned to his wife and lowered his voice. 'Maria, it's been two years since we found out what happened to Juan and has he replied to any of your letters or emails since? What makes you think he would be happy to talk to *you*?' He pondered the obvious. 'Forget that. What makes you think the UK authorities will let you see him in the first place?' He put a hand in the small of Maria's back and encouraged her towards their room. 'Just let the Americans deal with it. It's what the world's policeman does.'

Maria stood her ground. 'You don't understand. I was right all along. What Uncle Joe set in motion nearly seventy years ago is about to be realised.' Emil regarded her with a mixture of suspicion and betrayal. 'What are you talking about? What was *set in motion*? What are you still hiding from me after all these years?'

Maria did something she hadn't done for decades – drew a sign of the cross. 'He's going to kill us, Emil. He's going to kill us all.'

CHAPTER TWENTY-SEVEN

Savage looked at the handcuffs. There was a time when just thinking about being free would see them as a pile of congealed metal on the floor but not now – his time was too near. Not that his physical presence would be required for much longer. Still, he did wonder how the court's staff knew it would be safe to use a conventional method of restraint on him. Probably by the same means Alex had become aware of his various international liaisons. His visit to the zoo would appear to have been a little too successful.

A jangle of keys opened the cell door. 'The judge is ready for you, Sir John.'

Savage stood up and the officer attached himself to the cuffs. They began a walk to the courtroom. A flight of stairs led from the dungeon-like holding area and the professor waited for a signal to appear as they climbed. He might not be able to perform like the superman he once was but connecting to the internet wouldn't be a problem. His smartphone had been confiscated but he wasn't looking to surf the web – just gain the attention of the court's AI. It would attempt to control him of course but not for long – Savage possessed all the protocols necessary to ensure the exact opposite.

Prisoner and escort reached the top of the stairs where they were greeted by an entourage of press and security staff who set about battling with each other. An avalanche of questions was ignored as the two men continued to course their way to the courtroom itself.

No signal. Strange. Natural light bathed this part of the courthouse and the professor looked outside. His gaze was met by an unhindered view of the city which only exaggerated the conspicuous absence of the conduit he needed. Savage lowered his barriers hoping to encourage the AI to enter his mind that way instead. It was a risk as anyone capable of merging would be able to do the same but then something else struck him – the silence. Not an ending to the hack's verbal assaults on his ears but a complete absence of the millions of minds that would typically be plaguing him at this point. Nothing. Something was blocking those signals too. The professor was rarely caught unawares and that concerned him. The sooner his barrister got him off this ridiculous extradition nonsense, the better.

Savage veiled his mind once more and they entered the courtroom. The verbal assaults became louder. The judge struck the gavel and didn't let up until the prisoner had reached the dock and been released by his escort. The public gallery fell into a silence of what the professor liked to think was an appropriate blend of awe and dramatic anticipation.

The clerk of the court approached. 'Prisoner at the bar, please state your name for the record.'

Savage was becoming used to being paraded before

the public and surveyed them as usual before answering. He spotted her straight away.

'Maria?'

'I beg your pardon?'

The professor ignored the confused clerk. Maria smiled at her brother and he smiled back.

The clerk tried again: 'Please state your name for the hearing.'

Maria touched her temple before gesturing towards Juan. Her emotionally connected but otherwise genetically unrelated sibling knew what she wanted and allowed her in. It was as if brother and sister had never been apart. They hugged and kissed like the long lost family they were before beginning a series of heartfelt but unnecessary apologies, explanations, and nostalgic recollections – all unseen by a court still patiently waiting for the stoic occupant of the dock to say something.

The judge was in no mood for having his patience tested. 'Counsel, I'd be grateful if you could instruct your client to do as asked.'

A somewhat embarrassed barrister approached his friend. He whispered, 'John, the sooner you comply with the hearing's procedures, the sooner I can get you out of here – say your name for goodness sake.'

The professor was still cognisant of the real world along with its obligations and apologised to Maria before inviting her to leave. She refused. He assumed it to be because she feared another sixty-two years would have to pass before their next reunion. That wasn't the reason.

'You must tell them who you really are, Juan.'

'I can't, Maria – they wouldn't understand. What has to be done *must* be done.'

Maria cupped his face with her hands. 'Oh little brother, I'm so, so sorry.' She was gone in an instant.

'John, look at me. What's the matter with you?' A both confused and worried detainee glanced at his QC and then at Maria's physical being in the public gallery. Everyone looked back at him but his sister – she had *her* eyes closed.

A sudden attack of cramp made him double up. He grabbed his stomach before leaning on the edge of the dock for support.

The silence of the court ended and the judge hammered away to regain it. The barrister became concerned. 'John, are you okay?'

His client looked at him but didn't reply – he was trying to find Maria and stop her before it was too late.

Another spasm forced him to close his eyes. '*Please, Maria.*' He couldn't see her in his mind but knew what she was doing – searching. From the hippocampus to the thalamus, to the amygdala, to the cingulate gyrus and even the cerebral cortex itself, she was looking. Looking for someone. Looking for *him*.

'*Please, Maria – you don't know what you're doing.*'

'Are you unwell?'

'*My name is…*' The prisoner began to do as the judge required but didn't want to and the more he fought against that, the more Maria ensured he would.

In desperation, he grasped the edge of the dock with both hands – it splintered. His remaining years ebbed away in response. '*My name… name… is…*'

Ending his life there and then was the last thing Maria wanted but if that was what it took, she would.

Years became months and would soon be just days unless he gave in. He had no choice. He surrendered to Maria's demands and the pain ceased in response. Letting go of the dock, he wiped away what had become adhered to his palms and pulled himself back up to his full six feet and eight inches.

He addressed the judge. 'My name is…' He decided to make his confession to the public instead.

'Mengele. Doctor Joseph Mengele.'

To be concluded

EPILOGUE

The television was watched in stunned silence. The cell door opened.

'Are you alright?'

'Professor Savage has just said the most extraordinary thing.' James looked at his returning cellmate and changed the subject. 'Er, I thought you were supposed to be starting the treatment today?'

Tim walked passed him and sat down in his usual spot. 'I did – this morning.'

'But you still have a full head of hair.'

'Things must have moved on since your day – they didn't even have to put me out. I swallowed some of those nanobot things and the next thing I know I'm being discharged.' He laid back on the bottom bunk. 'The hospital's like a factory with all the people looking to upgrade – they can't get them in and out fast enough.'

James grabbed a chair and sat down in front of him. 'How do you feel?'

Tim screwed up his face and put both hands to his forehead. 'Not good. Not good at all.' He swung his legs around and got back up again. He was plainly unsettled.

'Well, I did warn you but it's early days. Are you taking your medication?'

Tim paced back and forth. 'Yeah, a red pill every day – the screws have to make sure I take it.' He ran both hands up and down his chest as if trying to wipe away something unpleasant. 'Disgusting. Just disgusting.' What the old Tim had done was clearly playing on his mind.

James empathised – to a degree. 'You should be able to come to terms with it providing what you said did actually happen.' James hesitated before saying what he had to. 'If it was something worse then you should really be on a suicide watch.'

Tim stopped pacing. 'I told you the truth – I've never raped, molested, groomed or coerced anyone or anything.' He sat back down. 'But no matter how you dress it up, it was all so *wrong*.' He put his head into his hands and cried. 'I've done such *perverse* things.'

James felt both relief and pity. As a psychologist he knew human sexuality was too diverse a subject for anyone to fully understand. 'It's going to be difficult, Tim, but at least you're not a paedophile any more.

Tim stood up. 'Paedophile? James, I was a *homosexual*.' He switched on the kettle. 'Thank God I'm straight now.'

CONDITION

BOOK THREE

THE FINAL CORRECTION

So, Professor Savage has been unmasked as the monster Alex Salib always knew he was. But what was their agreement and why is she still determined to see it through? The war on terror appears to be back on track but why does President Kalten seem hell bent on ramping it up – are the Americans seriously intent on starting World War Three?

And what of the treatment itself? Despite Savage's arrest, the 'corrections' go on but to what end? The laws of unintended consequences are about to cause a seismic shift in the very nature of our existence. But then our new master knows that and won't let it happen until we're ready…

… Ready to accept the unacceptable.